Is There Anybody There?

C E J Waterson

Chris Waterson

Foreword

The strengthening wind grips the tall firs, their lower branches entwine, as though performing some kind of ritual dance. Naked silver birch stand poised, elegant, and unbent against the icy blast. Old oaks groan in protest, their roots stretched and their vibrant foliage ripped from their branches, swirling like flames through the forest. The dense undergrowth jostles for position, straddling the paths to a previous existence, concealing the dark secrets of this ancient woodland.

Chapter 1

Ruth was humming away to the music on the radio as she put the finishing touches to the soup she was making. She felt happy and looking forward to spending the next few days with her family.

In her early sixties, Ruth was a petite brunette with a healthy glow about her, having spent a good summer mostly in the garden or on the golf course. She and her husband, Nigel, had recently retired from their lucrative business as estate agents, and were thoroughly enjoying spending more time together.

They had rented an old farmhouse in a small holiday complex on a country estate to celebrate their wedding anniversary. It was their fortieth, a ruby wedding and an opportunity or excuse (whichever way you wanted to look at it) to get everyone together. The occasion had been in the planning for months and now the time had come.

They were expecting all three of their children. Nick, their eldest and nearly forty years old had, until recently, enjoyed a totally bachelor existence, living in a fairly cheerless apartment near the city. Like his father in many ways, he worked hard and was steadily making his way up the ladder at the Stock Exchange. He had met his girlfriend, Carys at a party in the summer and this would be the first opportunity to introduce her to the family.

Emma, their only daughter, graduated from university with a degree in art and design. She had carved out a successful career for herself and travelled all over the world promoting her original ideas. She met her husband Rob on a trip to the States and there had been an instant connection. They married soon after meeting, and now had two little girls, Sophie and Paige.

Their youngest son Jack was a bit of an afterthought, although Ruth couldn't say any of her children were planned, but certainly Jack was more of a surprise than the others. Only in his twenties, he was considerably younger than Nick and Emma. He started working in the family business when he left school, but being 'in property' was not for him. He had enjoyed being a holiday rep for a while, which took him all over Europe, but currently he was backpacking his way around Australia. The trip was supposed to take only a year, but he had been away for over two and there was no sign of him returning.

Communication had been sketchy and, although Ruth and Nigel received e-mails regularly, actual contact was rare. Seemingly, Jack found work in hospitality or farming to fund his adventure and never once asked his parents for money.

On one of the very few occasions when they had managed to speak, Ruth mentioned their upcoming celebration and said how much she would like him to be there. He had agreed to come home at once, without any hesitation, which left Ruth wondering why she hadn't asked him to come home before!

She finished blitzing the soup and put it to one side for later. She was extremely pleased with just how much she had managed to achieve in the short time they had been at the farmhouse.

It helped having the place to herself, Nigel having gone for a walk. She had fondly blown him a kiss and waved from the window, as he went through the gate into the little lane that led to their temporary home. By his side was their black Labrador Brodie, wagging his tail at the prospect of discovering new places.

Ruth glanced at her watch and saw it was twelve thirty. Plenty of time to check the rooms and make sure everyone has what they might need.

Everywhere was clean and tidy, although Ruth knew it was unlikely to stay that way once the family arrived. The old farmhouse was beautifully refurbished; the kitchen had been extended, making it a very big social space with bi-fold doors leading out to a neat courtyard garden.

The lounge was comfortably furnished with cushioned sofas surrounding a log burning stove. Large windows let in plenty of light during the day and heavy curtains would keep it cosy at night.

An imposing staircase led from the living room to a spacious landing and two big bedrooms, both with en-suite. One overlooked the garden at the rear and the fields beyond, the other faced the lane and the woods hiding the village.

Ruth busied herself going from room to room, even laying the table for dinner thinking that would be one less job to do later. Nigel had already laid the fire and would light it on his return so there would be a warm welcome.

She crossed the courtyard to a converted barn. Here a contemporary, open plan kitchen and living room straddled a flight of stairs leading to a bedroom on a mezzanine floor above. Ruth thought Nick and his new girlfriend might like to stay here as it would give them some privacy. She drew curtains and switched-on table lamps, knowing it would probably be dark when they arrived.

Adjoining the barn, were the stables; again, converted and refurbished to a high spec with many of the original features and much of the charm skilfully being retained. Ruth admired the clever use of space and knew Emma and the little girls would love it here. Open-plan living was again evident, but a bright hallway led to the main bedroom and bathroom on the ground floor. A little wooden staircase led into what had originally been the hayloft and Ruth immediately thought her son-in-law Rob would have to watch his head. She had bought a couple of little surprises for Sophie and Paige, which she left on their beds, together with a few age-appropriate puzzles and games she had selected from a collection in the main house.

With nothing more to be done until later, she returned to the kitchen. The sun was still streaming in through the windows, increasing the warmth from the Aga. She could hardly wait to see everyone and had a genuine feeling of excitement. What a very special time this was going to be.

Chapter 2

Nigel had followed a narrow footpath signposted to the village, which ran along the edge of the woods. At the end of it, he had come to the main street and easily found the pub.

He was early, as the walk had only taken him twenty minutes, but the young barman welcomed him cheerily and Nigel ordered coffee. A roaring fire in the grate was already creating a warmth and he sat in an easy chair beside it with Brodie at his feet. Watching the barman, Nigel could not help thinking the young chap looked somewhat out of place. From the few words already spoken, Nigel detected a Scottish accent, but it was the straggly ponytail, piercings and tattoos that seemed incongruous.

"Where do you hail from?" he asked inquisitively.

"Dundee. I came here two years ago, as a temp for the summer, but got offered the job and have been here ever since! Are you new to the village or just visiting?"

"We're staying on the Bentley Estate for the weekend. I walked down to see how far it is as we're hoping to have lunch here tomorrow?"

"Of course, would you like to see a menu?"

Nigel was browsing through the choices, when a few more customers arrived. Judging by appearances, they were farmers, clad in warm jackets and sturdy boots. Most of them acknowledged him with a 'how do' or comment about the weather, but one came over to make a fuss of Brodie and introduced himself as Jim Caldwell. They shook hands and Jim sat down in another chair by the fire. His dark, swarthy complexion and calloused hands were evidence of spending many hours working outdoors.

"It'll get busy in here shortly, with it being Friday," he said amiably. "We like to grab a pint and a pie. Have you come far?"

"Home is only an hour away, but we've rented the holiday lets on the Bentley Estate for the weekend."

Another man came to join them who Jim introduced as his brother, Bill. Taller and broader, with a mop of fair curly hair, Nigel would never have guessed their relationship. He ordered a pint and sat with them as they ate their lunch.

Talk turned to how much farming had changed and the need to diversify. Some years ago, the brothers had lost a whole herd of dairy cattle to foot and mouth and more recently, a few of their cows had tested positive for TB and had to be destroyed. These disasters were demoralising, but somehow, they had managed to carry on; renting a few fields for grazing and using the rest of their land for growing crops.

Nigel and Ruth had also worked hard for many years building their own business, but the power of the Internet had severely tested their personal approach for selling houses and, seeing the 'writing on the wall', they had quickly branched out into managing rental properties and also made a few sound purchases themselves to let out.

Sharing this information about how they too had to think of different ways to keep their business going, Nigel then mentioned the impressive conversions where they were staying.

This prompted Jim to ponder, "We've got several barns and outbuildings we don't really use any more. It would be good to convert them so they're habitable and don't just fall into disrepair."

"Great idea, but probably too expensive," Bill said, "worth considering though."

"Would you like me to take a look?" Nigel offered, "I've done a few renovations and could give you an idea as to whether they're viable."

Both men smiled and nodded in agreement, Jim saying enthusiastically, "That would be really helpful. When could you have a look?"

Nigel checked his watch and thought he would have plenty of time for an initial assessment and be able to get back to the farmhouse before the family arrived.

"No time like the present," he said.

Chapter 3

Ruth stepped out of the bath and wrapped herself in a fluffy robe, twisting a towel over her damp hair. She wandered through to the bedroom and was surprised to see the bedside clock showing two thirty. Could that really be the time? She quickened her pace; it wouldn't do for the family to arrive and her not be ready to greet them.

She dried herself off and selected a pale blue angora jumper and navy trousers and wondered why Nigel had not returned. Maybe he had and she hadn't heard him, but there was no sign of him or Brodie in the living room or kitchen.

She filled the kettle and put it on the hob. Finding a teapot and mugs, she set a tray. She had made a chocolate cake the day before and took it out of its tin. The girls loved chocolate cake and, decorated with butter icing and smarties, it was bound to be a winner!

She was just warming the pot when she heard a car drive in and before she could get to the door, it flew open and in rushed Sophie and Paige with their two lively springer spaniels, Tilly and Meg.

The girls were super excited and hugged Ruth with gusto whilst the dogs dashed about sniffing everywhere. It was bedlam, but Ruth revelled in it and made a big fuss of them all. Eventually, she was able to untangle herself and greet her daughter.

"This is going to be fun!" she said as she gave Emma a hug and a peck on the cheek.

"I think it is!" Emma laughed and stepped aside as Ruth was swallowed up in a bear hug from Rob.

He was a giant of a man at over six foot four, whilst Emma was like her mother, tiny with short dark hair and elfin features, but their relationship was far from contrasting. They were a good team and very obviously in love.

They all sat round the table with Ruth pouring the tea and Emma cutting the cake. The dogs were searching about for Brodie, but when Rob called them over, they came obediently and laid down.

"Where's Nigel?" he asked.

"I'm not actually sure;" Ruth replied candidly, "he set off on a walk some time ago to the village. I thought he'd be back by now. He's probably got chatting to someone at the pub. He'll be back soon."

They had almost finished tea when another car pulled into the driveway.

"It's Uncle Nick," the girls exclaimed together, sending the dogs into a frenzy of barking, as they all headed for the door.

"You've made good time," Ruth said as Nick got out of the car.

"The roads were pretty clear considering it's Friday and we were both able to get away promptly," Nick replied. "This is Carrie Mum," he added introducing his new girlfriend.

"Very pleased to meet you," Ruth said warmly as they shook hands.

Nick did all the other introductions and whilst Rob helped Nick unload the car, Ruth led the way back into the farmhouse.

Carys was very attractive and Ruth could see immediately why Nick had taken to her. She was really quite tall, certainly taller than Ruth or Emma, with blonde hair swept up into a messy ponytail. She was wearing jeans, a blue stripy top and a bright green quilted jacket. She was trendy, but not too sophisticated. She wore little make-up or jewellery and by completing her look with sensible boots, she was dressed for a weekend in the country. Both Ruth and Emma warmed to her right away and offered what was left of the cake and a cup of tea.

The little girls were unusually quiet, clearly observing the newcomer and weighing up her 'auntie potential'.

Rob and Nick joined them and everyone was very convivial until Nick enquired, "Where's Dad?"

With all the activity, Ruth had pushed her anxieties to the back of her mind. Now, looking out of the window at the dimming light, she felt uneasy, but didn't want her concern to alarm anyone.

"I expect he's got chatting to someone and hasn't realised the time, but if he's not back before dark, I'll be having serious words with him."

"What time did he go out?" asked Nick.

"About half eleven, I think. He took Brodie for a walk to the village to check out the route and see what the pub's like."

"That's ages ago - it's nearly four. Surely, he should be back by now?" Emma said full of concern. "Rob, why don't you and Nick drive down to the village and see if he's still there?"

"Sure, we'll call you if we find him, but if he shows up in the meantime, tell him he's missed out on buying us a beer!"

The door closed behind them and Ruth got up to clear the cups. She was really worried now, although she knew she shouldn't panic. Nigel often went out walking for hours. Maybe he had got a bit lost and was taking longer than he anticipated. He always liked to take a circular route, rather than returning by the same path, and this had resulted in him taking lengthy detours on quite a few occasions. She always insisted he took his mobile with him, but he usually had it on silent and rarely answered when she called. However, she thought it might be worth a try and wished she had thought about it before the boys had gone looking for him. She pressed the call button and within a few seconds heard the familiar ring tone. Clearly Nigel hadn't taken his phone with him - it was sitting on a side table in the living room on charge.

"Don't worry Mum," Emma said, "he'll be back before you know it," although she wasn't actually convinced. Her Dad

11

was normally very reliable and she knew he would have wanted to be there to welcome everyone.

"Something smells good," she said trying to change the subject.

"It's beef casserole." Ruth said vaguely.

"Oh lovely! Mum's casseroles are amazing," Emma told Carys. "I don't suppose there's apple crumble for afters by any chance?"

"There is," Ruth responded as she went to the window to look out anxiously at the darkening skies.

Nigel is running late, but reckons by taking the short cut Jim and Bill have suggested, he will be back to the farmhouse before the family arrive. Brodie needs the walk and so does he.

Going to the farm to see the disused buildings had been worthwhile. Structurally, they all looked sound and not at all dilapidated. Nigel was able to convince the brothers of their potential and the three men had discussed the possibility of a joint venture. Subject to planning permission, the conversions could be let out as rental or holiday homes, or even sold to people looking to buy. Nigel had willingly agreed to be their project manager, should they decide to go ahead, and was genuinely excited at the prospect.

The fields, normally full of cattle, were now empty for the winter and Nigel and Brodie easily make their way across to the woods. The wind is getting up and it feels chilly, but there is still plenty of daylight.

As he goes through the final gate and turns to close it, Nigel can see the brothers still watching them. He gives them a wave and a 'thumbs up' before entering the wood.

It's quite dark, but the footpath is obvious and Nigel hurries after Brodie who is confidently trotting ahead.

Chapter 4

Nick drove slowly down the lane, there being a few potholes that were difficult to see in the growing dusk. Rob kept an eye out for Nigel, particularly when they came to the signpost to the village. There was no one to be seen on the road and even when they entered the main street, very few people were about.

They found the pub without any problem, parked up and went in. Three people were sitting at the bar on high stools and two couples were relaxing in leather chairs facing the fire. A dining area could be seen through a stone archway where tables were laid, ready for serving evening meals.

Rob and Nick fully expected to find Nigel, deep in conversation, with Brodie at his feet patiently waiting to continue their walk, but they could see immediately he wasn't there and went to the bar to make enquiries.

"Aye he was here," the young barman said, "he came in early and got talking to a couple of the locals. They all left together a couple of hours ago."

"Any idea which way they went?" Nick asked.

Realising their concern, the barman replied, "I did overhear bits of their conversation - is your dad into property?"

"Yes, he is why?"

"They were discussing a possible barn conversion and I think he was interested. Maybe they went to take a look."

"Would you know where the barn is?"

"At the farm I presume, which is away up the back road, about a mile or so." The barman went with them to the door to indicate the direction.

Back in the car, Rob made a call to Emma, "Your dad was at the pub, but he left with a couple of locals and it's possible he's gone to their farm to look at a barn for conversion. We're on our way there now to see if he's still with them or if they know which way he went. Try not to worry Em."

Emma was seriously concerned, but didn't want to alarm her mother.

"That was Rob Mum," she said in a steady voice, "they think Dad maybe at a farm looking at a barn for conversion."

As she said it, she felt pathetic and was sure her mother would realise she wasn't convinced.

Ruth did, but in turn didn't want Emma or the girls to see her panic.

"Trust him to put business before pleasure," she said testily, "he's still not used to being retired and can't resist a business opportunity."

Carys had been unpacking and returned to the kitchen to find Ruth looking very worried and Emma doing her best to behave as if nothing was happening.

"Any news?" she asked softly.

Emma told her what little the boys had found out so far. Carys opened the bottle of wine she'd been holding and found some glasses. As she poured, she asked Ruth if they'd stayed at the farmhouse before.

"We haven't actually stayed here, but we've often driven through the village on our way to the country park for a walk. We only live an hour away."

Emma's mobile rang and she answered it immediately. It was Rob.

"Your dad's not here, but he was. The chap he's been with offered to give him a lift back, but he said he'd rather walk. That was well over an hour ago."

The path has narrowed and, with very little light penetrating the trees, Nigel is beginning to feel uneasy. He considers turning back the way they have come, but reasons they must be nearing the main footpath and determinedly pushes on.

Brodie retreats behind him, adding to Nigel's disquiet.

"It's OK feller, we'll soon be out of here," he says with more conviction than he feels.

Chapter 5

There's a knock at the door and everyone turns towards it expecting to see Nigel and Brodie saunter in. The dogs, tails wagging, are eager to greet whoever is there. When the door doesn't open and Emma and Ruth, their faces filled with anxiety, make no attempt to answer it, Carys steps forward and yanks it open, calling the dogs away. There, in the dim light, stands a young man with a rucksack.

"Jack!" Ruth and Emma say together.

Carys stands aside to let Jack into the room. He is tall and tanned with chiselled features, certainly not resembling Ruth or Emma or even Nick for that matter, she thought.

"Thank God you're here," Ruth said throwing her arms around him, "Nick and Rob are out looking for your dad - we don't know where he is."

"We're so worried," added Emma as she too gave her brother a hug.

The two little girls, who had been playing quietly, noticed the tenseness in their mother's voice as they came to greet their uncle. Sophie had been three years old when she had last seen Jack and Paige, only a baby. They stared shyly at him as he listened incredulously to what had been going on.

Nick and Rob returned and, after greeting Jack warmly, reiterated what the barman and farmers had told them.

"They met Dad in the pub," Nick said, "and took him to see an empty barn. They discussed various possibilities, but as Dad was anxious to get back here, they agreed to meet again after the weekend. Jim offered to give Dad a lift, but he was determined to walk, so they suggested a short cut across their fields and through the woods."

Everyone listened attentively to Nick and when he had finished, Rob added his thoughts.

"It may be Nigel has somehow strayed from the footpath and got lost or worst-case scenario, fallen and hurt himself. Whatever's happened, don't you think we should call the Police?"

"I think so," Emma said quietly, "it's the sensible thing to do. Make the call please Rob."

While Rob stabbed at his mobile, Jack paced back and forth, not able to keep still.

"I need to be doing something to find him," he said and began frantically looking in cupboards for a torch.

"Jack, let's wait for the Police," Nick said gently, "we don't know this area and it won't help if we get lost too."

Jack ignored his brother and continued his search. Nick did his best to comfort Ruth, who by this time, was visibly shaking and obviously very upset.

Emma tried to distract the little girls, who were close to tears.

"Let's get you both in a nice warm bath," she suggested and led them, with very little persuasion, across the yard to the stables.

Rob was still on the phone to the Police, carefully answering questions with as much detail as he could possibly give.

Carys didn't know what to do. She felt completely helpless. Robotically she filled the kettle and put it on the hot plate. She wondered if she should take the casserole out of the oven, but hoped maybe someone would want to eat later.

Rob ended his call.

"They're on their way, but they may not be able to do anything until the morning."

Ruth broke away from Nick with an agonised cry and went to look out at the inky blackness.

"Oh Nigel, where are you? Where on earth can you be?"

All she could see was her own shadow and the reflections of her sons and Rob behind her. The kitchen was now bright with lights, but the feeling of warmth and cheerfulness she had enjoyed earlier had gone, and was replaced by fear and an utter dread of the unknown.

Chapter 6

The call was unexpected, but not unwelcome. Kevin had been squatting in the back of the van for three shifts now, looking at the same block of flats, and was quite glad of the excuse to take a break. He knew, indeed he could smell, there was drug use and dealing going on, but he had yet to identify the offenders. It was frustrating, but with patience, he would get the evidence and make some arrests.

Kevin enjoyed his job. Even in this rural community, there was always something happening and rarely, were two days the same. He had been a sergeant for five years and was happy to be at the sharp-end. Indeed, he found policing the small towns and surrounding countryside made life varied and interesting.

The observation he'd been on for the past few days had given him the opportunity to watch the local residents coming and going and gather information to get closer to the offenders. His van had one-way glass in the doors at the back, and he devised a cover in case anyone looked in at the front. A hard hat was on the passenger seat with a high viz jacket and overalls on hooks across the space behind. Kevin hoped this would convince any inquisitive passer-by that he was a builder and not an undercover cop.

Being six foot two, he didn't find it easy sitting still for hours with his knees up under his chin, but he had fitted a mattress over the floor and strategically placed cushions around the sides, so with careful manoeuvring, he could change his position regularly and remain fairly comfortable. He worked alone most of the time, which suited him as there was no distraction from the task in hand, nor the temptation to talk and be overheard.

This preference for his own company was significant in his private life too. He found relationships difficult to keep when his hours were unsociable and his whereabouts taboo. He hoped one day to meet someone who would understand, but for now, he concentrated his efforts, and most of his time, on doing his job.

He took a final look through the rear window and listened intently for any passers-by before crawling through to the front. It was quiet, too quiet for a Friday night, and no doubt as soon as he left, it would liven up. He would have liked to get out and stretch his legs before driving off, but didn't want to arouse the curiosity of anyone who happened to be looking out of a window. He started the engine and moved off without lights and maintained radio silence until he was further down the road.

The wind slaps low branches into Nigel's face and brambles snatch at his jacket and tear at his hands as he tries to force his way through the undergrowth. Blindly, he battles on with Brodie panting anxiously at his heels. He can no longer offer any reassuring words. All he can do is convince himself they must almost be out of the woods.

Something grips his ankles, pitching him forward; he plummets to the ground, hitting his head hard; knocking him out.

Chapter 7

Headlights shine briefly in through the window.

"The Police are here," Rob says as he goes to open the door with everyone's eyes following him.

On the doorstep, a young man with a stubbly beard, wearing jeans and a bomber jacket stands there in the dimming light. As he enters the room, he politely removes his baseball cap and shakes Rob's hand. He introduces himself as DS Kevin Spencer and the young woman, who had come in behind him, as WPC Gina Ford.

"Gina is a Family Liaison Officer," he explains, "and will stay here to relay any developments as they happen. She'll need to ask some very pertinent questions to totally eliminate any logical explanation for the disappearance of Mr Harrison. I hope you won't mind?" he says, quietly addressing Ruth, who dumbly shakes her head.

"I'm afraid we're a bit thin on the ground. I've two men searching along the footpath from the lane to the village and I've asked them to interview the barman at the pub in case he's remembered anything since you spoke to him earlier. I went to see the farmers before I came here and they're concerned and mystified about Mr Harrison's disappearance. They're getting a few people together, who know the area, and will organise a search from the other side of the wood. I wonder sir," he said looking at Rob, "would any of you feel able to assist with the search this end until more help arrives?"

Immediately Jack, who had managed to find a torch and was already shrugging himself into a warm coat belonging to his dad said, "Lead on."

"Shall we take the dogs?" asked Rob, "They know Nigel and his dog very well. Maybe they can help us find them?"

"Good idea, but please keep them on leads so we see where they go. The woods are pretty dense and we don't want to lose track of them."

"No problem," replied Rob, calling the dogs to him. Excited about getting an unexpected walk with tails wagging, they obediently sit as their leads are slipped over their heads.

Handing them to Jack, Rob says, "I'll just check on Emma and the girls. I won't be a minute."

Nick looked at his mother, who silently nodded and gestured for him to go. He glanced at Carys who gave him a little smile and said, "We'll be fine - take care."

The men stepped out into the darkness, momentarily letting in a cold blast of air and the sound of rustling leaves being whisked around the courtyard. The wind was getting stronger; it was going to be a wild night.

Rob went across to the stables where he found Emma helping the girls into their pyjamas.

"Will you be OK if I help with the search for your dad?"

"Of course, but please be careful. I'll take the girls across to the main house and stay with Mum."

Rob fondly kissed her with a hug and said good night to his two little daughters; both very solemn.

"Do you think you'll find Grandad in the dark?" whispered Sophie.

"I don't know Sophie, but we're going to try."

He turned quickly away and headed for the door before Emma and the children could see his doubts.

Nick and Jack were waiting for him with the dogs and Kevin joined them, having retrieved a couple more torches from his car.

"We'll need to stay as close together as possible," he said, "normally I'd be saying we should spread out and cover as much ground as we can, but in the dark it's not advisable, especially as none of us are familiar with the area. Hopefully, the farmers will have been able to make a more thorough search. Unless we find Mr Harrison quickly, I suspect we won't make much progress tonight, and we'll have to start again in the morning."

No one made any comment as they made their way to the footpath, each silently praying Nigel would be found safe soon.

When they reached the second footpath leading through the wood, the undergrowth was so thick on both sides of the path, they had to remain in single file, shining their torches in a continuous arc around them in an attempt to penetrate the darkness. They walked slowly and in silence, listening for any sound that might lead them to Nigel and Brodie. They could hear nothing other than the wind ripping through the trees and the dogs panting as they pulled on their leads, eager to be let loose.

Eventually Kevin said, "Maybe we should call out. He could be trapped somewhere and might hear us."

"DAD!" yelled Jack immediately. *"Where are you? Can you hear me?"* There was desperation in his voice and it broke with emotion.

Nick called out too, "Dad - are you there?"

They stopped, straining to listen for any answer, but heard nothing, only the howling wind. They continued making their way slowly forward, stopping every so often to call again. Rob even tried to imitate the whistle Nigel used for Brodie in the hope the dog might at least show up, but to no avail.

After what seemed like an eternity, they saw flickering lights through the trees and heard faint voices. Suddenly, there was a deafening crack followed by an immense thud that shook the ground. A large tree had blown down somewhere very close. They were all paralysed with fear, even the dogs were stunned into silence.

Kevin was immediately concerned for the safety of the other search party and called out, "Jim are you all OK?"

There was no immediate reply, but then Jim was heard to say, "Everyone's alright, but it's a huge tree and blocking our path. I don't think we can go any further."

Shouting above the storm, Kevin agreed they could do no more. He couldn't actually see the tree, but he knew it was only a few feet ahead of them. He tried not to imagine what might have happened if any of them had been further along the footpath.

"Go home Jim," he shouted, "and thank you all for your help. We'll start again at first light."

Kevin led the way out of the woods, very much quicker than how they had entered. The brothers and Rob knew it was futile to argue; there was nothing more to be done tonight. The weather was against them, as well as the dark, and there was a very real danger more trees would come down. They reached the relative safety of the lane and, with shoulders bowed against the wind and driving rain, headed back to the farmhouse.

Nigel is shaken awake by the ground shuddering. He cries out as clods of earth fall on his face and he vainly attempts to spit the soil from his mouth. He goes to sit up, but excruciating pain seers up his arm and grips his chest. He slumps back to the ground in agony; his eyes close as he surrenders again to unconsciousness.

Chapter 8

Emma and the little girls are curled up on the settee under a duvet in front of the log burner that Carys managed to light. Emma had tried putting the girls to bed upstairs, but they kept coming down in floods of tears saying they were scared. She had relented and put a DVD on for them, hoping they would fall asleep.

Carys had made copious mugs of tea and coffee, most of which had been left untouched. She had taken the casserole out of the oven expecting to see it completely dried up and inedible, but although everything was well cooked, it wasn't spoilt. She had asked Ruth and Emma if they would like anything to eat, but neither of them had any appetite. The little girls had warm milk and biscuits.

WPC Ford had quickly become a comforting presence and said they were to call her Gina. She had asked some rather direct questions and Ruth had stoically answered them. There seemed to be no underlying reason for Nigel's disappearance.

Gina explained that normally, when an adult went missing, a search might not be instigated straight away. More often than not, the missing person would be taking time out from a situation they were finding difficult to cope with, and simply needed to be alone for a while to sort things out.

Clearly, there was nothing bothering Nigel, as far as Gina could tell from Ruth's answers. They were well off financially and the business was continuing to thrive, even without their daily input.

When Rob reported Nigel missing, he had been emphatic that it was totally out of character, and this had resulted in the early search. Hearing the rain blasting against the window, Gina truly hoped Nigel Harrison would be found safe and well tonight and soon be back with his family.

Sophie and Paige had eventually fallen asleep, and Emma and Carys took them upstairs to the second bedroom, gently tucking them into the comfy double bed, hoping they wouldn't wake until morning.

Ruth sat in an armchair beside the log burner, staring into the embers, the shadows from the flames flickered in the dim light. She could not believe what was happening. Within a matter of hours, what should have been a fun-filled family get together, had turned into the worst possible nightmare.

Emma too was fixated on the fire. She sat in a corner of the settee with her legs tucked up and her arms wrapped around her body looking utterly miserable. The room was warm, but she was visibly shivering.

Conversation had ceased some time ago, when all discussion about the most likely and unlikely scenarios surrounding Nigel's disappearance, had been exhausted.

Carys got up from her armchair and drew the curtains to shut out the spiteful weather, but the wind whistled down the chimney and the rain was still beating against the windows.

"Can I get you anything?" she asked Ruth, who just shook her head unable to answer. It was obvious to Carys that this lovely lady, whom she had only just met, was being tortured by the situation and she felt powerless to help. She looked across at Emma and got the same response.

Going through to the kitchen, she found Gina quietly talking into her mobile. As she filled the kettle, yet again, in the hope that Ruth and Emma would at least drink a cup of tea, Gina finished her conversation.

"I'm afraid there's no news. They haven't found Mr Harrison and the weather is too bad for them to continue their search."

Carys shook her head in disbelief. How could someone just disappear into thin air? She was warming the pot when the door flew open and the dogs belted in, closely followed by the men, letting in an icy blast of cold air before the door was firmly shut on the dreadful night. They all looked weary, but the brothers particularly, had the same haunted look on their faces as their mother and sister.

Carys' heart went out to Nick. She was already very fond of him and could not bear to see him looking so worried. Jack was angry and frustrated at having to abandon the search. He threw his coat on the floor and punched his fist in his hand before slumping into a chair. Rob put his hand on Jack's shoulder, sending the dogs to their beds and sitting down beside him.

Silently Carys poured the boiling water over the tea in the pot and set up mugs.

Nick put his arm around her saying, "I think we need something stronger than that."

"There's only wine," she said and found some glasses.

Nick poured a good measure into each with a shaky hand and offered them to Rob and Jack who both downed the red liquid in one go.

Kevin had been murmuring to Gina, but now said, "I have to pick the PCs up from the pub. If the barman or any of the regulars have any more useful information, I'll let you know. I need to write a report and make sure we get a proper search going first thing in the morning. Gina will be staying if that's OK?"

Only Nick responded and thanked Kevin for his help as he went with him to the door. Once again, there was an icy blast of cold air as Kevin stepped out into the night.

"Goodnight sir, try to get everyone to eat something and rest if at all possible."

"I'll try, but I think this is going to be a very long night."

Nick closed the door and joined Rob and Jack sitting at the table.

Carys took mugs of tea through to the living room. Emma was still shivering and barely acknowledged her when she placed the tea on a table beside her.

"Would you like me to run you a hot bath?" she asked, picking up on Emma's earlier suggestion to the little girls.

"Thanks," Emma said simply and looked across at her mother, "Would you like one Mum?"

Ruth hardly seemed to hear the question, but shook her head and continued to stare into the fire.

Returning to the kitchen, Carys found the men each with a plateful of stew. She had put some jacket potatoes in the oven earlier and was relieved to see they were still edible.

"I think your poor mum needs to go to bed," she said quietly to Nick. "Emma's going to have a hot bath, but neither of them are coping very well."

Hearing that, Nick and Rob rose from the table and headed through to the living room. Jack continued to stab at the meat left on his plate. He was eating just for the sake of it - he wasn't hungry and could barely taste the food.

"Thanks for doing this," he grunted.

"It's your mum's casserole - she'll be glad it hasn't gone to waste."

There wasn't much left in the dish, but Carys offered to share the remnants and a jacket potato with Gina.

Jack excused himself and got up from the table, putting his empty plate in the dishwasher and disappearing into the living room.

Carys and Gina continued eating in silence. When they both had finished, Carys cleared away the plates and put the empty casserole dish in the sink to soak.

"Would you like a bed for the night?" she asked Gina.

"If there's one free; otherwise, I'll be fine on a settee somewhere. I'm used to snatching a few hours whenever I can."

"I don't think there'll be much sleeping tonight and I imagine the family will want to stay together, so if you want to sleep in the barn or the stables, you'll be more than welcome."

Carys didn't really know what to do herself. She wanted to be there for Nick, but he was consoling his mother and staying strong for his sister and younger brother. She felt as though she was intruding on their despair and should give them all some space.

"Why don't we go over to the barn and make you comfortable? I'll come back and see how they're all doing in a little while."

The fierce wind was twisting the trees and leaves swirled in circles around the two women as they hurried across the courtyard.

The barn was warm and welcoming, despite there being no fire in the grate. With the curtains having been closed earlier and the table lights switched on, the vast open plan living area was a surprisingly cosy space.

Gina admired the surroundings and said, "I'll be fine on this huge settee - it's almost as big as my bed at home."

"I'll find you a duvet and pillows," Carys said and went out again across to the stables, knowing there would be two spares from the little girls' beds.

When she returned, Gina was on her mobile, listening intently. She mouthed, "Thank you," as Carys left the bedding and, feeling she should make herself scarce, went upstairs to run a bath.

Rob and Jack too were rummaging for duvets and blankets to make up temporary beds in the farmhouse. Emma and Ruth had been persuaded to go upstairs and rest, even if they couldn't sleep. The little girls were still curled up in the big spare bed and Rob quietly closed the door, leaving a night light on in case they woke up.

Returning downstairs, he found Jack pouring a generous glass of wine and nodded when Jack offered him one. He found biscuits and cheese, which he put on a tray. He knew they had little appetite, but it had been a very long day and was going to be an even longer night. He settled the dogs in their baskets and carried the tray into the living room, where he found Jack cradling his wine and staring morosely into the fire. The room was warm, but Rob put another log in the burner and he too sat reflecting on the events of the day.

How could all this have happened? Nigel had set off on an easy walk to the village and stopped at the pub, where he had met two farmers. They had taken him to see some disused outbuildings to assess whether they were suitable for conversion. He had refused a lift, even though he was running late, and taken a shortcut back to the farmhouse and vanished! Rob didn't know the area, but from what he'd seen of the woods and the footpaths, he found it difficult to believe Nigel had got lost. During their initial search, it had been impossible to deviate from the track because of dense undergrowth, but maybe in daylight, other paths would become apparent.

He looked at Jack who was clearly suffering. What an ordeal this must be for him. His expectations of a warm welcome and wonderful family reunion, completely shattered.

"We have to stay positive," Rob said quietly, although he felt far from confident that all would be well by morning.

Jack nodded miserably, unable to say anything. He was so afraid of what they would find next day. Surely, if his dad was alright, there would have been some sight or sound of him and where was Brodie? He was missing too.

Just then, they heard the back door open and the dogs delightedly whining to greet whoever was there. Jack leapt to his feet and strode through to the kitchen hoping to see his dad and Brodie safe and well, but it was Nick who stood on the doormat, having been across to the barn.

"I'm sorry Jack, there's no news I'm afraid," he said, seeing the disappointment on his young brother's face. "Gina has been in touch with Kevin who says there's been no further developments. The barman doesn't remember anything else and none of the locals can add any further information. Dad's description has been circulated and hospitals have been notified. That's all they can do."

Jack returned to slump in front of the fire and Nick followed him through to the living room, shaking his head at Rob who was under a duvet on the settee.

"No news I'm afraid. I've sent Gina over to the stables for the night. I hope you don't mind, but she may as well have a proper bed rather than sleeping on the sofa. I'll stay in the barn with Carrie; there's not really room enough for all of us here."

"No worries Nick. I'll keep an eye on things."

"Thanks Rob. I'll be back first thing. Good night."

Nigel comes to; it's dark, very dark; he can't see a thing, but feels the damp, icy chill seeping through to his bones. He is cold, so cold and his involuntary shivering makes every part of his body twitch painfully. He is in agony and, as yet another spasm grips his chest, he cries out in desperation, "Is there anybody there?"

All he hears is the whine of the wind as his choking cries go unheard above the violent storm and he slips, once more, into oblivion.

Chapter 9

No one expected to sleep that night, but somehow everyone managed to doze, even if only for a matter of minutes.

Rob was woken from his fitful sleep by Sophie and Paige.

"Has Grandad been found?" Sophie wanted to know.

It took Rob a minute or two to recall the events of the previous evening and sadly shook his head, "No, not yet Sophie, but we're going to look for him again today once it's light."

The little girls ran to the window and pulled back the curtains to reveal the darkness and their reflections against the dim lights in the room.

"I'm hungry," Paige said, "can we have some breakfast, Daddy?"

Rob rose from the settee, stretching his stiff limbs and headed for the kitchen. He didn't really notice whether Jack was still where he'd been all night in front of the fire, but immediately missed his dogs coming to greet them.

Before he could say anything, both girls were asking, "Where are the dogs?" and went to the window to look outside.

"I can't see them in the yard, but maybe someone has let them out or taken them for a walk?" suggested Sophie.

"Run up and check on Mummy girls, will you? Maybe she couldn't sleep and has taken them down the lane. *Utterly ridiculous,*" he was thinking to himself. "*it's not daylight and the dogs wouldn't expect a walk in the dark!*"

Rob filled the kettle distractedly and put it on to boil, listening to the girls running up the stairs. He went through to the living room and wasn't really surprised to see the chair Jack had occupied, empty. "*Maybe he's gone out with the dogs, but in the dark? That's irresponsible, knowing how worried everyone would be.*"

He carried on up the stairs. He could hear Emma talking to the girls calmly, but then heard her voice change to concern, "Oh no, where's Grandma?"

The door to the bathroom opened and a very tousled Jack appeared.

"Have you seen your mother?" Rob asked him.

"No why?" replied Jack clearly puzzled.

"She's not here!" Emma said close to tears.

Rob led the way hurriedly downstairs and, as he made for the back door, he noticed Ruth's coat was missing from the hooks and the dogs' leads.

"Let's just check out the barn and stables before we panic," he said, trying to sound calm.

He ran across the courtyard and without bothering to knock, opened the barn door and called out, "Ruth are you here?"

Almost immediately he heard Nick's voice, "Rob what's happened - why are you looking for Mum?"

"She's not in the house and my dogs have gone, so I was checking everywhere before we report her missing too!"

Nick and Carys appeared at the top of the stairs hastily pulling on clothes. As they reached the bottom, Rob was already halfway across the yard again to the stables. Without knocking, he barged in, but was stopped from shouting out when he found an astonished Gina sitting at the kitchen table, nearly dropping the mug she was holding.

"I'm sorry to barge in," he stammered, "but Ruth is missing from the house and I'm just checking everywhere."

"She's not been in here. How long has she been gone?"

"We don't know," Rob said anxiously, "she must have crept passed me and Jack and somehow taken the dogs out of the house without waking us up."

"She'll have gone looking for Dad," Nick added as he stepped in behind Rob, "she's out of her mind with worry."

Gina knew, even without looking at the tension in their faces, there would be no point in trying to persuade them to wait for Kevin and his search party. It was still dark outside and she could see a torch light bobbing about in the yard. No doubt that was Jack impatient to get going.

"Kevin is on his way, but if you want to go and look for your mum, I won't stop you. I'll go over to the house and stay with Emma and the girls and let Kevin know what's happened. Just please be careful."

Rob, Nick and Carys joined Jack, and Gina watched them go through the gate into the lane. The wind had lessened, but it was still cold and she hoped Ruth hadn't gone far and they would find her straight away.

When she entered the farmhouse, her heart went out to Emma and the little girls; clinging to one another and sobbing loudly. She went to them and put her arms around them, desperately trying to give them comfort with reassuring words. When eventually their tears subsided, she led them through to the living room and tucked them all up under the duvet on the settee. She set about clearing the grate to relight a fire and put the kettle on to make hot drinks.

Jack led the way down the lane dodging the potholes and shining his torch ahead.

"*MUM?*" he yelled, but there was no answer.

All four of them were jogging now, feeling the need to find Ruth as quickly as possible. Jack was the first to reach the footpath leading to the village and stopped for the others to catch up.

"Do you think she'll have gone down there or carried on?"

"We don't know, so let's split up," Rob suggested. "Nick, you and Carrie check the rest of the lane and Jack and I'll search the footpaths. If she's with the dogs, it's more likely they'll have gone this way. I would whistle for them, but I don't want her pulled off her feet if they're on leads or abandoning her if they're not."

"Right," Nick said, "have either of you got a phone?"

"I have," Rob replied, "and I'll call you if we get anywhere. Mind how you go."

Using the torches on their mobiles, Nick and Carys continued along the lane, whilst Rob and Jack took the footpath until they came to the track through the woods. Should they follow that path or carry on to the village? Before they could decide, they heard a rustling in the undergrowth and the next minute Tilly, one of Rob's spaniels darted into view, tail wagging and clearly delighted to see her master.

"Mum, Mum!" Jack shouted immediately, convinced Ruth would not be far away, but there was no other sound and no sign of Meg either.

"Where are they?" Rob said to his dog. "If only you could talk."

Tilly dived back into the bushes, but there was no way Rob and Jack could follow. Rob whistled and the dog reappeared.

"I think they must be in here, but I'll call Nick and tell him to head into the village at the end of the lane and come back on this footpath. That way, we'll have searched both ends and we can carry on through the wood."

Rob made the call and they started walking down the track. They hadn't gone far when his phone rang.

It was Nick, "We've found her, but she's in a bad way. Carrie is phoning for an ambulance."

Jack barged passed Rob and ran back along the footpath, quickly disappearing from view. Rob whistled and called for his dogs. Again, only Tilly responded as he too went back the way they had come. As he reached the lane, day was breaking and he could just make out the three figures crouched down at the end of the drive. He hurried towards them and was relieved to hear a siren in the distance. Help was coming, he prayed it wouldn't be too late.

Before the ambulance arrived, Kevin's police car appeared and he jumped out looking very concerned. Gina had rung him to let him know about Ruth being missing too and he was mightily relieved to see she was safe, although it was very obvious from the abnormal angle of her foot, she would need to go to hospital.

When Rob reached the group, he heard Carys saying, "Take it easy Ruth, we'll soon get you sorted. Just lie as still as you can."

"I'm so sorry to cause all this fuss. It was so silly of me to let the dogs out. I thought they would just go as far as the field and come back to the house, but they took off down the lane, so I went after them - such a stupid thing to do!"

Trying to reassure his mother, Nick said, "We're just so relieved to find you Mum, but you need to go to hospital. It looks as though you've broken your ankle and you must be freezing."

Ruth was shivering, despite Nick and Carys having put their coats around her.

By now the entire search party had arrived and Kevin was directing operations. It had been a cold windy night and it was imperative to find Nigel as soon as possible.

Jack was thankful his mother had been found and now wanted to help in the search for his father. Kevin was more than grateful to have him along as the more people looking, the more likely the search would be successful.

The Paramedics confirmed that Ruth had indeed broken her ankle, which they immobilised before she was carefully lifted into the ambulance. Carys offered to go with her and Nick thanked her gratefully, as he felt he would be more use on the search.

Rob was anxious to get back to the cottage to see if Emma and the little girls were alright. He had managed to make a quick call to let them know Ruth had been found, but the whole situation was very distressing. He was also hoping his other dog, Meg had managed to find her way back to the farmhouse and be none the worse for wear. It was strange she hadn't shown up with Tilly; they were normally inseparable.

Chapter 10

There were about twenty officers deployed for the search, plus the farmers who had rallied again. Kevin was left in charge, although he now had the backing of more senior officers. It was important to coordinate the areas still to be explored and make sure no obvious places were overlooked.

The dense undergrowth either side of the footpaths made it almost impossible for the search party to look anywhere else, but there were two police dogs methodically sniffing through the trees and under bushes.

Rob had re-joined the search, having been reassured by Emma that she and the girls would be fine. There was still no sign of Meg, and Rob had left Tilly at the cottage so she wouldn't distract the trained dogs from doing their job. He was feeling wretched and looking at Nick and Jack, knew they were both feeling the same.

What an awful situation they were in and how would it all end? The longer the hunt for Nigel went on, the less chance there was of finding him fit and well. He must be somewhere between the farm where he had gone to look at the barns and the estate, which really had to centre on the woods. There was nowhere else he could have gone without finding his way to a road and safety. It was unimaginable to think he would even consider leaving his family without explanation. So, where was he? Where was Brodie - would the dog not have found his way back to the farmhouse and raised the alarm? He was intelligent; a typical Lab who had been easy to train and utterly devoted to Nigel. It was this thought that made Rob believe the dog wouldn't have left him, no matter what.

He couldn't help thinking about his own dog too. Meg had never caused him any concern until now. Being more nervous than Tilly, she had managed to stay out of trouble, even when they were puppies.

He was torn from his thoughts by Jack shouting, "*Dad, Dad where are you?*"

The poor man was almost hysterical and had fallen to his knees sobbing like a child. Nick crouched down beside him, his arms around his younger brother doing his best to comfort him, but unable to hide his own despair.

Rob went to them both and with a hand on each shoulder said, "Come on boys, let's go back to the house, we're really not helping here."

Kevin saw what was happening and hoped Nick and Jack would do as Rob suggested. He was finding their emotions hard to witness and by now, was wondering what they might find. It could be very unpleasant.

Without any more being said, Nick took Jack under the arm and helped him up and together with Rob, made their way back along the footpath and out of sight.

The search continued with plenty of encouragement for the dogs from their handlers. The wind had died completely and as the morning went on, the sun managed to poke its way through the dark clouds and weakly penetrate the tall trees.

The sound of chainsaws could be heard and Kevin knew the farmers were already hard at work trying to clear the path.

Eventually the two search parties met at the fallen tree. It was indeed a big one and had taken down several others as it crashed to earth. The path was completely blocked and there was no way through, other than climbing over it, but the trunk was massive and that would take some doing.

When there was a lull in the noise from the sawing, Kevin shouted out, "Jim, how're you doing?"

"The tree's huge and there's a lot of debris to be cleared before we can attempt to chop it up."

"Can we get the dogs round it anywhere?"

"Doubt it. It's pretty thick and we haven't managed to get along to the roots yet where there might be some space."

Kevin turned to the dog handlers, "Would either of you be able to climb up and get over to the other side?"

"Sure," said one of them immediately. He was a burly chap, but surprisingly athletic as he scaled the tree trunk. At the top, he turned to call for his dog, a huge German Shepherd. The other handler braced himself against the tree as the dog leapt on to his back, using this as a platform to clamber up the rest of the way. Clearly, they had done this before and were well rehearsed in overcoming obstacles. The dog waited patiently at the top whilst his handler carefully climbed down the other side to the ground, where he got into position for the dog to jump down.

Kevin realised there was nothing more his party could do until the footpath was cleared and even then, it was highly unlikely they would be any more successful than the farmers.

He had asked everyone involved with the search to meet at the pub by twelve thirty for a debrief and further instructions if Nigel had not been found. With no reports of sightings, he knew the next step would be an appeal for information on radio and television. He left two officers at the tree to help clear the path and indicated to the others to follow him out of the wood. This included the other handler and his dog, a lively cocker spaniel, specially trained to find dead bodies, although this information Kevin and the handler kept to themselves.

At the lane, Kevin directed the men to continue the search around the farm buildings, including the fields beyond and sweeping back along the road at the top of the hill and across the farmland where Nigel was last seen. They should then make their way back down the road to the pub.

Meanwhile, Kevin would be meeting with his Inspector to arrange a wider search by helicopter and even horses to scour the countryside. If Nigel Harrison wasn't found today, it had to be assumed he could have gone further than the immediate vicinity. His description had already been circulated throughout the county, but with Emma able to produce a recent photo of her dad and his dog, details of their disappearance would now go national. Up to now, the hope had been he would be found and there would be no need to broadcast him as missing, but as each hour passed, that outcome was looking less and less likely.

Nigel's consciousness is brief. He can hear howling; he stares blindly into the pitch dark and remembers nothing. Unable to move, his entire being is numb and he can no longer resist the desire to sleep. He welcomes its nothingness and quietly slips away.

Chapter 11

Rob and the brothers had almost reached the lane when his phone buzzed. He quickly retrieved it, anxiously looking to see who was calling. It wasn't a number he recognised, but he answered it anyway and stopped to speak.

A man's voice responded to Rob's "Hello?"

"Oh hello, I think I've found your dog. It ran into my garden and frightened my chickens, but I think it's pretty scared itself."

"Oh, thank you. I'm so sorry if she's been a nuisance; she got out first thing this morning and I had no idea where she could be. Can I come and collect her?"

"If you would. I live at Priory Cottage next door to the church in the village. Do you know it?"

"I don't, but I'll find you. I just need to let my family know what's happening. Unfortunately, it's not only my dog that's been missing, my father-in-law and his dog are too. We've been out searching for them. I don't suppose you've seen any sign of them, have you?"

"I'm afraid not, but that would explain why there's all the Police activity here. Just come when you can, I'll look after her."

"Thanks, you're very kind. Her name is Meg – she's a bit timid and must have been spooked by something to run away. I'll get to you as soon as I possibly can."

Rob rammed the phone back in his pocket and ran to catch up with Nick and Jack. As they entered the driveway, they became aware of an old battered Land Rover parked just inside the gates.

"We've got visitors," Nick observed, "and I don't think it's the Police."

As they entered the farmhouse, Gina and Emma looked up from where they were sitting at the kitchen table with an elderly lady wearing a tweed jacket and headscarf.

The two little girls ran to Rob for a hug.

"This lady says we can stay," Sophie told her dad, "but I want to go home!"

"This is Marie Langton who owns the properties," Emma explained, "and she's kindly said we can stay beyond tomorrow if necessary; she has no other bookings until next weekend."

Marie Langton turned to the men and said, "I've only just heard what's happened and I'm so sorry. If there's anything we can do, please don't hesitate to ask. We're along the lane at Bentley Wood Manor. My husband has gone to see if he can help with the search, but if there's anything else we can do, you know where we are. I'll pop by again later in case you need anything."

"Thank you very much. Your kindness is greatly appreciated," Emma said as she went with Marie to the door.

Gina looked at the three men and could see they were all severely affected by not knowing what had become of Nigel. Kevin had texted earlier to say they were on their way back and she should be prepared to give them all support. Sadly, she had had to deal with these situations in the past and was well used to people ranting, mostly at the Police, in pure frustration when a search was proving fruitless. Strangely, these people were quiet, but she knew emotions could kick in at any time and she was prepared for this happening.

Without saying anything, she quietly made a pot of tea and set mugs and milk out for them to help themselves. She looked in the fridge, which was still very well stocked, as no one had really eaten much since yesterday afternoon. She took out some cheese, chutney and tomatoes and found some rolls in a bag that were still perfectly fresh. She put plates and knives out and hoped they would eat.

Sophie and Paige were still clinging to Rob, and Tilly was wrapping herself round his feet.

"Meg has been found," he said dully, knowing no one had really given her absence much thought. "She's with a man who lives in the village and I need to pick her up. Will I take the girls with me Em?"

"Please do Rob. They could do with some fresh air."

Her tone wasn't lost on Rob; he knew she wanted him to give them a break from what was going on and it would give her a chance to discuss their next moves with her brothers. They couldn't stay here indefinitely and it would be just as well to return home and at least give the girls a level of normality.

He and the little girls left the farmhouse with Tilly at their heels.

Once the door shut behind them, Emma turned to Nick and Jack and said, "I think Rob and I should take the girls home. We can't do anything here and it's just too upsetting for them. I'll wait and see what's happening with Mum - we should hear from Carrie soon."

"I've just had a text," Nick said looking up from his phone. "Mum has broken her ankle quite badly and will need an operation to pin it. Obviously, she'll be in hospital for a while, which is maybe just as well as she'll be properly looked after. I feel pretty useless too, but we need to stay for now in case Dad turns up."

"Why hasn't he been found?" Jack said suddenly with such venom that everyone looked startled. He thumped his fist on the table and ran his fingers through his hair before slumping into a chair looking utterly defeated.

"Everything that can be done is being done," Gina said calmly, trying to reassure them all, but knowing full well, the longer the search went on, the less likely it would result in a happy ending. "You all really need to eat something or at least have a hot drink. Please, have some lunch, you need to stay strong and positive."

Emma poured the tea and Nick sat down at the table.

"Come on Jack," he said trying to encourage his brother, but Jack remained where he was and kept silent.

Chapter 12

Rob found his way to Priory Cottage and parked up outside. As he got out and went to open the door for the girls, he heard Meg barking and next minute, she was haring down the garden path to greet them. They opened the gate and made a fuss of her; her tail wagging as she went from Sophie to Paige, licking their faces in recognition.

Rob looked towards the house and saw an old man standing on the doorstep, smiling at the sight of this joyful reunion. He beckoned them to come in. Rob opened the boot of the car and immediately Tilly jumped out to greet her sister in typical doggy fashion, but with a few firm words, the dogs obediently leapt into the car. Rob ushered the little girls through the gate to thank the kind man for looking after Meg.

Fred Green was a sprightly 79-year-old who had lived in the village all his life. The cottage inside was cluttered, full of memorabilia, particularly photos of his family and pets. An old sheepdog got out of its bed and walked stiffly towards them, gently waving its tail in greeting.

"Steady Gem," Fred said quietly, "we're not used to visitors, so it's a bit overwhelming for her."

The girls stroked Gem carefully until she returned to her bed and Fred offered to introduce them to his chickens. They went into the garden where the hens were pecking about freely. A chicken coop stood in a corner of the garden, set in a wire pen, but Fred explained he just let them roam around during the day.

He suggested to the girls they look for eggs, and gave them a basket each to collect any they found. Whilst this was keeping them occupied, Fred drew Rob to one side.

"Did you say your dog only went missing this morning?"

"Yes, very early, before it was light. My mother-in-law let the dogs out and, when they didn't come back, she went looking for them. Unfortunately, she fell and has been admitted to hospital with a broken ankle. Our stay here has been a nightmare!"

"I'm so sorry to hear that. I take it the Police haven't found your father-in-law yet?"

"Sadly, no," Rob replied, "he was last seen entering the woods and hasn't been seen since."

Fred listened with interest and then said, "It's probably nothing, but late last night when I went to bed, I heard a dog howling. At first, I thought it was the wind, but it had dropped a bit by then - it was definitely a dog. It sounded weirdly mournful and made me look out the window. There was a single shaft of light shining through the cloud and something flew up from the trees; it was most odd; then it disappeared. I know it sounds a bit far-fetched and I've never really believed the stories before, but it did make me wonder. The woods are said to be haunted by a huntsman, who died when his horse fell. They say his hound buried him, but no grave was ever found nor the horse or the dog."

This information perturbed Rob as he tried to rationalise what Fred had told him, but in truth, he really did not know what to make of it.

"Would you mind if I tell the Police what you've said?" he asked Fred.

"Of course not, if you think it will help."

Rob called Sophie and Paige, who were still searching around the garden for eggs. They had found four and carefully placed them in a box Fred gave them to take home. Thanking him for everything, Rob and the girls got in the car and drove away, waving until he was out of sight.

Stopping at the pub, Rob went to see if Kevin was in the mobile unit, now set up in the carpark to coordinate the search.

There was just one officer inside the cabin, manning communications. Rob explained who he was and asked if Kevin was about.

"He's gone back to the search, but I can get him on the radio for you."

"Thanks, but I need to get back to the farmhouse. Could you ask him to contact me there please? He has my mobile number, but I'd like to see him if that's at all possible."

"Of course, I'll let him know."

Chapter 13

Rob found Emma in the stables. There were tears streaming down her face as she sadly packed their belongings into bags. He took her in his arms and tried to comfort her, but she only cried more, letting go of all the misery of the last twenty-four hours.

When the sobs lessened a little, she said, "We have to take the girls home Rob. It's not fair on them - they don't really understand what's going on and I'm afraid for them if something dreadful has happened to Dad."

Rob didn't argue, but he still had hope that Nigel would be found and tried to encourage Emma to remain positive. He had left the girls at the farmhouse, where Gina was trying to rustle up something for them to eat.

Jack was refusing to leave and said he would stay there alone if necessary. Nick felt they should go to the hospital to see their mother and he intended bringing Carys back for the night. Rob had thought they would all stay for the weekend, but he could see Emma was determined to return home. He knew it made sense; there was nothing they could do and at least they would be nearer to the hospital where Ruth had been admitted. What a ghastly situation and how was it all going to end?

He took the packed bags and put them in the car, letting the dogs out into the field for a short run. As he was putting them back, Kevin arrived on foot and a little out of breath.

"I got your message - what's happening?"

Rob repeated what Fred had told him, even though he thought it was probably old wives' tales. Kevin raised his eyebrows, but did not dismiss it as nonsense.

"Quite a few places in the area are shrouded in folklore and superstitions, so it doesn't entirely surprise me, but I've always thought it's just that - make believe to attract visitors! I just wish we could find something that will lead us to Mr Harrison. There's nothing - no sign of him or his dog anywhere, but we'll keep looking until dark and let you know if we get anywhere."

"Thanks - I'm actually taking the family home. We feel it would be better for the girls, and Emma is so upset being here and not able to do anything. At least we'll be closer to the hospital to visit Ruth. I think Nick and Jack are staying, at least until tomorrow."

"The search has widened on the ground and there's a helicopter in the air. Let's hope we get a break soon."

Gina came to the back door and offered them both something to eat, but Kevin said he should get back to the search. He assured Rob that he would give the Inspector in charge the information and promised to drop by again later.

Emma appeared in the courtyard, having dried her tears and, putting on a brave face, headed into the farmhouse with Rob.

Chapter 14

Kevin made his way back through the wood to the centre of the search. Chainsaws had been going all morning, carefully cutting through the huge tree, which was slowly being removed in an effort to uncover any clues that could possibly explain the disappearance of Nigel Harrison.

A helicopter was hovering over a much wider area than could be covered on foot, but as much of it was dense woodland, it was the locals, knowing the village and the surrounding area, who were able to help make the investigation very thorough. Horses and quad bikes were proving to be extremely efficient, searching along bridleways and over vast expanses of farmland.

Kevin knew he had done his best in the circumstances, but having not found the missing man before now was very worrying indeed. In some ways he was relieved when his senior officer had taken over, but also disappointed that he had not managed to bring the investigation to a satisfactory conclusion. As sometimes happens in these situations, he could not help but get emotionally involved, and witnessing the family's torment, had been distressing. He was thankful to be allowed to stay on the job however, and contributed in a real way by liaising with the Police, locals and of course the family.

Right now, he was helping to shift the huge trunk as it was being sawn up. The footpath was clear, but what remained of the tree either side also had to be removed to eliminate any possibility the man or his dog were somehow trapped underneath. It was hard work and difficult to do because there was very little clearing, so the logs were put in wheelbarrows and taken to the nearest field and dumped.

The farmers had worked tirelessly all day, alongside those officers who had completed their search areas. It was essential to remove the tree before nightfall, so everyone just kept going.

Chapter 15

Rob, Emma, and their little girls had left to go home. They would be stopping at the hospital to see Ruth, and Emma would stay there if necessary. Nick was also going to the hospital, not only to see his mother, but to collect Carys. He had asked Jack if he wanted to go with him, but Jack had refused. He didn't want to leave in case their father was found.

So, it was just Jack and Gina left at the farmhouse. Gina had already put her bag in her car, not really sure of her next move. She may well be asked to stay with Ruth at the hospital, but for now she thought Jack really should not be left alone. She busied herself tidying up after their lunch, whilst Jack sat slumped at the kitchen table idly flicking at his phone.

"Fancy a cuppa?" she asked him.

"No thanks. Shouldn't you be somewhere else?"

"No, I'm supposed to be here until told otherwise."

"Do you think they'll find my dad?" Jack asked her bluntly.

"I don't know Jack, but I do know they're doing all they possibly can. I also know it must be very hard for you not knowing where he is."

"I should've come home sooner," Jack said berating himself. "Actually, I should never have left in the first place. I'm so selfish - I know my parents didn't want me to leave, certainly not to go travelling all over the place, but I had to find

60

out for myself what life is all about, or at least that's what it felt like at the time. I couldn't breathe; I had no life of my own; I was expected to follow in everyone else's footsteps and I wanted to make my own way. Now I wish I'd stayed working for Mum and Dad and been thankful, instead of careering about all over the world. I had everything, but needed to escape – why? I threw it all away and for what? I've not really achieved anything and I know I've probably disappointed my parents and maybe Nick and Emma too, but I didn't care - all I thought about was myself!"

The sobs came then, and he buried his head in his hands unable to control his feelings of guilt and sorrow.

Gina had come to think of Jack as the deep, quiet one. He'd said very little during the time she'd been with the family, but recognised this outburst as a good thing. She put her hands on his shoulders and said, "Let it go Jack. You've nothing to feel guilty about. None of this is your fault; it's happened and there's nothing you or anyone else could have done about it."

Jack turned to Gina then and put his arms around her waist, burying his head in her bosom. She didn't resist and gave him comfort until the tears abated, then she gently pushed him away and smiled, "I'm not sure that's included in my duties here, but in the absence of anyone else..."

"Thank you," he said simply and rose from the chair to look out the window at the darkening sky. He realised he may have overstepped the mark with Gina, but he wasn't embarrassed about it. He had needed someone and she'd been there for him at that moment.

"You're here for them now and that's all that matters," Gina said quietly.

Jack took a deep breath and turned to her, "I need a drink. Can we go to the pub?"

"I don't see why not. We need to let Nick and Carrie know where we are and I'll have to report to the Unit. They'll need to post someone else here."

Her job was to support the family, but she knew they would want someone at the farmhouse in case, by some miracle, Nigel Harrison returned. She was also hoping to be relieved of her duties overnight, so she could go home, shower and get a change of clothes.

"We'll go in my car," she said, as they put their coats on and left the farmhouse, locking the door behind them.

Chapter 16

Nick arrived at the hospital and found Carys, reading a story to the little girls, in a tiny waiting room next to the ward where Ruth had been admitted.

"Hello girls," he said, peering round the door, "how's Grandma doing?"

"She's got her leg in a sling to keep it up until she has an operation to mend it," Sophie informed him. "She has to stay here so the doctors and nurses can look after her."

Carys smiled at Nick. The girls had been very concerned about Ruth when they had first arrived, but the Staff Nurse took the time to explain to them what was happening and they seemed to understand and be less upset. Carys had offered to look after them, so Emma and Rob could talk to Ruth without interruption.

"Your mum's in the side ward next door," she told Nick, "she's doing alright, but seems a bit confused. They've had to give her pain killers, which might be the reason, but she was very dazed after her fall. She couldn't remember where she was when we were in the ambulance, and kept saying she didn't know what had happened. I explained to the Paramedics and the A&E staff about your father being missing and they've all been very kind. She's in good hands and the best place right now."

"I'll go and see her, and then I'm taking you back to the barn for the night. I had a call from Gina - she and Jack are in the pub and I've said we'll join them for something to eat later. I won't be long." With that, he went to see his mother.

Almost immediately, Rob appeared and told the little girls he was taking them home.

"Emma is staying with her mum for now;" he said to Carys, "we'll come back later to pick her up. Thanks for looking after these two."

"No problem. I just wish it was a happier occasion."

Sophie and Paige dutifully said thank you too and gave Carys a hug. Their little world had been turned upside down and Rob and Emma were doing the right thing by taking them home. They would one day come to realise what had taken place, but for now it seemed sensible to shield them from the grim reality.

Carys waved them goodbye and helped herself to another cup of water from the cooler in the corner of the room. She was struggling to control her emotions and was on the verge of tears. She had become totally immersed in this family who were being tormented, not knowing what had become of Nigel. Because of this tragedy, she had got to see all sides of them in a matter of hours. It was obvious how closely bonded they were, even Jack who had been missing from their lives for a few years. She could only imagine the hell they were all going through, but empathized by thinking about her own family and how utterly devastated they would be in such circumstances.

She also came from a loving environment. Her parents were childhood sweethearts and did everything together. She could barely remember a cross word between them and they had always been so supportive of her and her sister. Both girls had been encouraged to follow their dreams and be independent from a young age.

Carys had left her home in Swansea, South Wales when she was nineteen to go to University in London, studying politics and journalism. She quickly realised the diversity of politics was not for her, but writing stories was fascinating. She was good at it and even before getting her degree, she was selling articles to newspapers and magazines.

Carys was immensely proud of her roots and where she came from. Her parents lived in a three-bed semi in a quiet cul-de-sac on the edge of the town, which is where they'd been for almost the forty years since they married. It was this last fact that gave Carys a lump in her throat and made her eyes prick with tears.

Nick appeared in the doorway and said quietly, "Are you OK?"

He could see she was upset and having just come from consoling his mother and sister, was very close to tears himself. Carys turned and, without a word, put her arms around his neck. He embraced her and silently they let the tears flow. They clung to each other fiercely, each trying to stop the other from drowning. Eventually, Nick pulled away a little, kissing Carys' salty lips. She wiped away his tears with her fingers and kissed him back. It was a defining moment without a doubt. To be going through this ghastly experience together had brought them closer and they knew, whatever happened, theirs would be a very special relationship.

Carys found a tissue in her pocket and dried her eyes, "Will I just go and say goodbye to your mum and Emma?"

"Please do - I know they both want to thank you for all you've done."

"There's absolutely no need, I just want to help."

She left him then with a fixed smile on her face in the hope that neither Ruth nor Emma would notice she had been crying.

The side ward where Ruth had been admitted had four beds in it, but only two of them were occupied. The other patient was an elderly lady who'd also had a fall and broken her hip. She was a cheery soul and hoping to be discharged within the next day or two, once a home care package had been put in place.

Ruth was propped up on pillows with her leg elevated a little. Carys thought she still looked very pale, but maybe not quite so gripped by pain. Clearly, whatever medication was being administered through the catheter on the back of her hand, it was giving her some relief.

Emma was sat in a chair beside the bed holding her mum's other hand. The look of consternation on her face was obvious and Carys felt for her. Not only was she having to cope with her dad's disappearance and her mother being in hospital, she was also having to decide what was best for her little daughters. Fortunately, she could rely on Rob's support and together they would manage the situation.

"I've just come to say cheerio for now," Carys said brightly as they both turned towards her. "Is there anything you need that I can bring tomorrow?"

"Thank you," Emma replied immediately, "I managed to pack a few things I thought Mum might need, but can I call you if I think of anything else?"

"Of course, don't hesitate - if there's anything at all I can do. See you tomorrow."

Ruth said nothing, but raised her hand to her lips and blew Carys a kiss.

Emma said, "Thanks for everything, you've been such a help."

Carys touched Emma's shoulder, blew Ruth a kiss in return and hurried from the room before her emotions took over again.

Chapter 17

Gina reported to the Inspector who was now in charge of the search. Dan White was a highly respected officer, always very thorough in his investigations and often produced good results.

Gina explained what was happening with the family and why she thought she should continue to keep Jack company, at least until his brother returned. Dan agreed and detailed a PC on night duty to stay at the farm for now. He was far from confident the missing man would be found safe and well. Too much time had already elapsed and it was very unfortunate that both the weather and short daylight hours had hampered the search. The root end of the fallen tree would have to be left until the morning, as heavy rain had made the ground very wet and slippery. Most of the huge trunk had been removed, leaving quite a crater, but nothing unusual had become evident.

Dan had initiated an even wider search and broadcast Nigel's unexplained disappearance on local and national radio and TV, as well as social media. Unbelievably, not one sighting had been reported. Nigel Harrison and his dog had seemingly vanished into thin air. Dan thought this was quite extraordinary and, with no leads whatsoever, had interviewed everyone again who had seen them, as well as conducting house to house enquiries, in the hope that someone would remember something previously missed. He knew he would have to face the family sooner or later, but for now thought it best to leave Kevin and Gina to liaise with them.

Chapter 18

It was early in the evening and the pub was fairly quiet. Neither Jack nor Gina had been in there before, so no one recognised them as having anything to do with all the commotion in the village. They sat either side of the log fire, enjoying its warmth and the hospitality on offer. At any other time, they would probably have had a lot to say, but just now they were both lost in their own thoughts.

Jack was nursing a pint of real ale, something he had missed on his travels. He was focussing on the flames and wondering when and how this awful situation was going to end. He would visit his mother tomorrow and maybe return to the family home. He knew everything possible was being done here and he couldn't really help. Until his dad was found, they had to concentrate on getting their mother through this harrowing ordeal. Easier said than done, when they were all suffering so much.

Gina could see Jack was struggling with his emotions, but realised there was nothing she could say to make things any easier. Dan had told her to go home for the night to get some down time as she had been on duty for nearly twenty-four hours. She would return first thing tomorrow and seriously hoped the mystery would be solved by then. She discreetly glanced at Jack and thought how vulnerable he looked. For all his bluster, she knew he needed his siblings to be there for him. They had both been incredibly composed throughout the ordeal and the support they'd received from Rob and Carys had been marvellous. This sense of unity reassured Gina that, no matter what, they would tackle the future together.

The barman came over to put another couple of logs on the fire.

"Will you be eating with us this evening?" he asked.

Gina looked at Jack saying, "I think that would be a good idea, but shall we see what Nick and Carrie want to do when they get here?"

"I think so, if that's alright?"

The barman smiled, "Nae bother," and went back behind the bar.

The pub was filling up and it was obvious that many of the people filing in through the door had been out searching for Nigel. Gina wondered whether Jack would find it too difficult if they started discussing the situation, but he seemed oblivious to his surroundings and just continued to stare into the fire. He drained his mug and looked across at her to ask if she would like another.

"No thanks, there's only so much soda water a girl can drink."

"You're off duty now though, aren't you?"

"Yes, but I still have to drive home this evening."

As Jack stood up to make his way to the bar, Nick and Carys appeared in the doorway.

"Good timing - what are you both having?"

"I'll have a pint,' Nick replied, "and a glass of red for you?" he asked Carys.

She nodded and went to sit with Gina.

"How is he?" she asked.

"Quiet. He hasn't said much at all since we've been in here, but he got very upset earlier. He's blaming himself for what's happened, but I tried to stop him thinking like that."

"Nick is much more upset than he's letting on. Ruth isn't saying much either, not even to Emma. She just sits staring into space - like she really doesn't know what the hell is going on."

"They need lots of love and support just now, but if Nigel isn't found soon, they're going to need even more in the future."

"What do you think the odds are of finding him alive?"

"I wish I knew, but to be honest, the longer the search goes on, the less chance there is."

Nick and Jack joined them with their drinks and a menu from the bar. No one was really hungry, but knew they should eat. They ordered burgers and basket food they could eat by the fire rather than sitting in the dining area.

Conversation was limited and mostly about the food. When they had all finished, Gina said she was heading home, but would be back first thing in the morning. The PC sent to the farm would stay, if necessary, but Nick reassured her the three of them would be fine. They needed time to talk and decide what to do next. He thought they should leave as planned unless anything happened to keep them. They could do nothing here and the family home would be closer to the hospital. Ruth would be having her operation on Monday and it was hoped she could be discharged after a few days.

Gina thought this would be best for everyone too, and certainly it would make it easier for her to support them all, especially as Carys would have to go back to town. Nick was intending to phone his boss first thing on Monday to ask for time off, which he knew would be granted given the circumstances.

Clearly, the two of them had managed to discuss how they moved on, but Gina could see Jack was still very distraught. She hoped Nick and Carys would be able to offer him the solace he so desperately needed.

Chapter 19

Carys had gone to bed, leaving Nick and Jack to reminisce and maybe express their true feelings about the ghastly situation they were in. Nothing could be resolved until Nigel was found, but talking about it all would surely help them to stay strong and remain positive.

She had dozed off, listening to the quiet drone of their voices. She was exhausted, having become very emotionally involved with Nick and his family. Their ever-increasing unhappiness was disturbing to watch and she could only hope their lives would get better soon.

She was woken by a light briefly shining in through the window. The curtains were drawn, but the beam was very bright and invaded her sleep. Momentarily, she had to recollect where she was and what was happening, and then immediately thought it must be a Police car coming to give them some news.

Getting out of bed she went to the window to look, but there was nothing there - no light, no car - no one! She was about to turn away, thinking she had dreamt it when she heard a dog howling and saw a flicker of light in the wood. As she continued her gaze, the moon shone down through a gap in the clouds and as Carys stared at it, something flew out from the wood, soaring up through the beam. She blinked several times, unable to comprehend exactly what she was seeing. Surely it was an owl or some other night-time creature? She had never actually seen an owl, but this looked much bigger than a bird.

As she desperately tried to fathom out what it was, the beam and the figure vanished. She was left staring out into the dark night and realised she was shaking.

Feeling too unnerved to go back to bed, she went downstairs. Nick hadn't come to bed, so she thought she would find him and Jack still talking, but they were both sound asleep. Nick under a duvet on the settee and Jack in the chair by the fire covered in a blanket with an empty bottle of wine on the table between them. She hadn't the heart to disturb them and tiptoed through to the kitchen, quietly shutting the door behind her. She put on the light and filled the kettle, not that she really wanted a drink, but she felt the need to be doing something ordinary to take her mind off her bizarre experience. She was still shivering, so she put her coat on and leaned up against the Aga, glad of its warmth, whilst she waited for the kettle to boil. She'd just filled a mug when the door opened and a bleary-eyed Jack appeared.

"I'm sorry if I've disturbed you, Jack. I couldn't sleep and came down for a drink."

"I can't sleep either. It's going to be another long night."

Carys offered him a drink, which he declined, filling a glass with water instead. She didn't feel she could say anything about her weird vision, but was grateful to have Jack's company for a few minutes until he said he was going to bed.

She stayed in the kitchen, feeling a little calmer and less shaky. Had she imagined what she had heard and seen? Maybe she was just overwrought, like everyone else, and her mind was playing tricks. She wandered through to the living room.

Nick was still asleep, quietly snoring. She sat in the chair Jack had vacated and looked at him with deepening affection. He must have sensed her presence and opened his eyes to find her staring at him.

"Can't you sleep?"

She shook her head in response and he lifted the duvet for her to get in beside him. The warmth of his body was comforting and any further theories about the apparition were dismissed.

Nigel can see a tiny speck of light; its beam getting bigger and brighter. He feels himself drawn, very gently, out of the dark, silent place he's lain in for so long.

As he emerges from the shadows, he can feel the warmth of summer sun on his face; its heat soothing his tortured body.

He hears whispering, and although he is unable to make out what is being said, he feels comforted and safe.

He is free from the deep, dark pit of pain and despair; he is free from the future.

Chapter 20

Nick and Carys are woken by the now familiar sound of a chainsaw. They are surprised to see it's daylight and that they'd slept for quite a few hours, despite all the drama.

Carys gets up from the settee and goes through to the kitchen to fill the kettle and put it on to boil once again. Nick gets up too and stretches his cramped limbs.

"That must be the last bit of the trunk they're sawing up. I wonder if they'll find anything. I want to know what's happened to Dad, but I'm dreading them finding him hurt or worse."

Carys goes to him and puts her arms around him, trying to give him comfort.

"Kevin will let us know as soon as they find anything and I know this is incredibly hard for you, but do try and stay positive. You're doing a fantastic job holding the family together and they really need you to stay strong."

"It all seems so unreal. I still can't believe what's happened."

Carys held him tighter and they stood locked in their embrace, sharing an intensity and determination to get through this impossible situation together. They hear Jack on the stairs and draw apart. He looks pale with dark circles under his eyes, but has obviously just come out of the shower and changed his clothes from the ones he had been sleeping in.

"Morning," he mutters, "I'm going to the wood to see what's happening. Are you coming Nick?"

"Jack I really don't think we should. The Police are trying to do their job and we'll be in the way. Kevin will come and tell us if they find anything this morning."

"And what if they don't find anything?" Jack challenged. "What then?"

"I think we should go home."

"Home's not home without Mum or Dad."

Jack slumped down on a chair at the table, burying his head in his hands, his shoulders tremulous with grief. Nick went to him and cradled him in his arms like a child. The sobs came then as both men wept in despair.

Carys felt she could not say or do anything to give them hope. Indeed, at that moment, she couldn't help them at all and with tears streaming down her face, ran upstairs and threw herself on the bed, desperately trying to muffle her crying.

Chapter 21

Kevin parked his car at the pub and checked in with the PC in the mobile unit, before heading along the road to the footpath and the wood. He should be off duty, but had willingly volunteered to help continue the search for Nigel Harrison.

He could hear the chainsaw already in action and was anxious to be at the scene when the last bits of the huge tree were removed. It had continued to rain overnight and there was still a light drizzle, but the canopy from the trees and the dense undergrowth had kept this end of the footpath fairly dry. As he neared the clearing, where the men had been working all weekend, the noise stopped. The silence was almost deafening; there was not a sound, not even from the birds. It was like the forest was holding its breath. Jim and one of the other farmers were tugging at the last of the roots still clinging stubbornly to the ground and refusing to budge. Kevin went to help them, but as he did so, the root released and they both fell backwards.

"Are you OK?"

"We're fine," Jim assured him, getting back on his feet. "That last bit was difficult, but it's out now and we can get it all cleared away so your people can take a proper look."

Kevin was surprised by quite how much space the tree had taken up; the root end had left a sizeable hole in the ground. He helped the men put the last logs into their wheelbarrows and thanked them for all their efforts. As they disappeared from view, he turned his attention to the footpath and its surrounding area. He was desperate to find something - anything that would confirm the missing man and his dog had at least been in the wood.

The path from the tree the farmers had used was obliterated by footprints. Indeed, the whole area was pretty churned up and covered in sawdust, making Kevin think it would be a tough job for the forensic team to find anything. He called the Unit to let them know the tree had been cleared and carried on looking.

On his own now, he became even more aware of the quiet. It was eerie and gave him goose bumps. He tried to ignore it and concentrate on looking for clues, but found himself half expecting someone to appear from the bushes. There was a definite presence and it was unnerving. Without meaning to, he found himself veering away from where the tree had lain and going back down the path towards the pub. Within a few yards he spotted hoof prints. At first, he didn't think they were odd at all, and presumed they belonged to one of the horses involved in the search, but then he noticed there were no others - just the one set, and then they disappeared! He walked back and forth looking to see if the horse had gone off the footpath, but there was nowhere a horse could go. How had he not noticed them on the way in? This was baffling and increased his suspicions that something very weird was going on.

Kevin was relieved when the DI joined him and he could show him what he had found. He also reminded him about what the old man had said and although Dan agreed it was all rather strange, he didn't seem that concerned and said they should leave it to the forensic team who were on their way. He suggested to Kevin he might see how the family were doing. Gina had phoned him to ask where she should be, so it would be useful to know what they intended to do.

In truth, Kevin was grateful for an excuse to get out of the wood and readily agreed. He would contact Gina as soon as he knew what was happening. As he made his way towards the lane, other officers were heading into the wood, including the cadaver dog and her handler from the day before. He would know soon enough if they found anything, but for now he was glad to be away from it.

Nick, Carys, and Jack were in the kitchen when his knock was answered. Clearly, they had eaten breakfast and, judging by the bags stacked at the door, were intending to leave.

He gratefully accepted an offer of coffee and sat down with them at the table, saying as he did so, "There's no news I'm afraid. The tree has been completely cleared, but there's nothing obvious to give us any clues at all about your father. Forensics are now involved, so perhaps they'll come up with something. I'm really sorry, I know this must be very frustrating for you."

Nick said quietly, "Thank you Kevin. We really appreciate all that you've tried to do for us."

"I wish I could have done more. Gina is back on duty and wondering where you'll be today. Are you leaving here?"

"We are. There's absolutely no point in us staying unless we can help in any way. We'll be heading to the hospital once we've packed up and then Carrie will go back to town and Jack and I will go to the house."

"I'll get Gina to meet you at the hospital then."

"How long will they keep up the search?" asked Jack. He was clearly struggling to maintain his composure and Kevin could tell he was probably dreading the answer.

"There's no set time limit and we'll keep looking until every possible avenue of discovery has been explored."

He didn't want to lie or give them false hope, so he simply didn't mention that inevitably, resources would be reduced over time. For now, everything that could be done was being done, but it wasn't much help that there'd been no sighting of Nigel Harrison or his dog since they entered the wood, and not to find any evidence at all was quite extraordinary.

Carys got up to clear the table and bag up the last of their belongings.

As Kevin went to leave, there was a knock at the door. Nick answered it and on the doorstep was Dan, very apologetic, but a couple of objects had been found that needed identifying. Nick stood aside to let him in and Kevin introduced everyone. Dan laid two plastic bags on the table. One contained what looked like a dog lead covered in mud and the other had a cap in it.

"Does anyone recognise either of these things?"

Nick shakily picked up the bag with the cap in it to take a closer look. It was hard to tell the exact colour as it was soaking wet, but he could just make out the logo above the peak.

"That's Dad's golf club, so it could well be his, but I can't say for certain as I don't remember ever seeing him wear it."

"Thank you and the other object? Could it be the dog's lead?"

"It could be, but I can't be certain. Where were they found?"

"The lead was just off the main path, but had been well and truly trampled on by the farmers going back and forth. It was just by pure chance one of the lads spotted the clip in the mud. The cap was found hooked on a branch. It could have been blown there by the wind or snagged from someone's head as they walked close by. Since the tree has been removed, another very narrow footpath has been discovered and this cap was hanging above it. A very detailed investigation of the area is now being carried out, so hopefully we'll find more clues."

"That means I'm staying," said Jack firmly, "we could be about to find Dad."

Immediately Nick said, "Jack, if they find anything, we can come straight back, but we need to go and see Mum. She must be worried sick about it all and there really isn't anything more we can do here right now. We're leaving today."

Jack looked as though he was going to argue with his brother, but instead left the room. Nick went after him, leaving Carys with the two Policemen.

"Sorry about that."

"No need to apologise at all," Dan reassured her. "You're all under a great deal of pressure. As soon as we have any more news, we'll be back in touch."

As he made for the door, he nodded for Kevin to follow who added, "Bye just now. Gina will meet you at the hospital, but if there's anything we can do here, please let us know."

"Thank you," Carys said simply, once again very close to tears. She watched them leave and when the door was shut behind them, busied herself in the kitchen not wanting to interrupt Nick and Jack, who could clearly be heard having a heated discussion.

Dan and Kevin stood in the driveway, only too well aware of the argument going on between the brothers. Hopefully, Nick would be able to persuade Jack to leave, at least until any other evidence was found.

"I would like you to take the bags for identification to the hospital," Dan said. "If you don't think Mrs Harrison's up to it, then please see if their daughter can confirm whether the cap belongs to Mr Harrison, and maybe she'll even recognise the lead. We don't have anything else to go on and we really do need to know they're linked to continue the search."

"Will do. It's been so tough on them and they've been remarkably brave throughout this terrible ordeal. I can't help thinking it's not going to end well, given the length of time Mr Harrison's been missing; but if only we could find something that will tell us what has happened to him - at least that might give them closure."

They started walking away from the farm. Raised voices could no longer be heard so they could only hope the issue had been resolved.

"It's certainly not been straight forward and I agree, it's unlikely we'll find him alive unless he's found somewhere else, but with no one having reported seeing him, I think that's highly unlikely. However, stranger things have happened and we must keep an open mind and carry on looking for answers."

They came to the footpath into the wood and said goodbye; Dan heading back to the scene and Kevin hurrying on to collect his car and get to the hospital.

Chapter 22

Gina was already at the hospital when Emma, Rob and the little girls arrived. She had enquired after Ruth, but hadn't been in to see her as she was sleeping after, what the nurse described as, 'a very restless night'.

Emma looked really pale, clearly not having slept much either, but managed a smile when she saw Gina. The little girls too were very quiet and Gina tried to distract them with the promise of a story from a book of their choice in the tiny waiting room. Emma gratefully left them with her and she and Rob went to ask after Ruth. They were told the same thing, but Emma was anxious to be there when she woke up and they quietly entered the ward.

The other patient had been discharged, so unusually, there were three empty beds and Ruth was the only occupant. They each sat in a chair, saying nothing, just watching Ruth peacefully sleeping.

A nurse came in to check on her.

"It's good she's resting now; she really was quite delirious last night. She only had a low dose of painkiller and mild sedative to help her relax, but she was almost incoherent. We'll need to check how she is when she wakes up."

As the nurse went to leave, Gina appeared and asked Emma if she could spare a minute. Emma went immediately thinking something must be the matter with the girls, but Gina was quick to reassure her.

"Kevin's here. He needs you to look at something they've found."

Emma went with Gina to the waiting room where the girls were now playing happily with a little dolls house. Kevin apologised for the intrusion and, not sure what Emma's reaction would be, took her to the nurses' office where they would have some privacy.

Emma looked terrified and Kevin did his best to ease her gently into what he was asking her to do. He produced the bags and explained where they had been found.

"Can you identify either of these things?"

He could tell Emma didn't want to look at what he was showing her, but hoped she would recognise the items, then at least they would have some clues, however tenuous, about Nigel Harrison's disappearance.

"Please, just take a look. I really don't want to ask your mother, but we do need to know."

Emma glanced down at the bags and Kevin did not miss her sharp intake of breath.

"That's Dad's cap."

He guided her to a chair, before she fainted as clearly, she was overcome by this discovery.

"Would you like me to get Rob?"

She merely nodded, her eyes brimming with tears.

Ruth was still asleep when Kevin quietly opened the door and beckoned to Rob. Briefly, he explained what had happened and took Rob to the room where Emma was still sitting staring at the bags and their contents.

Kevin asked the nurse on duty to give the couple a few minutes and went to find Gina. Without alarming the girls, he said, "It's a match. I'm just going to let Dan know."

Gina nodded, but said nothing. She knew this was by no means conclusive, but at least it was a start to finding out what had happened.

Chapter 23

Dan received the news from Kevin and the search intensified, particularly along the narrow path now being uncovered. Dan had called on the help of the farmers again and two of them were slowly hacking back the dense undergrowth. The sound of activity in the wood was resounding across the countryside with more urgency than ever.

Nick had persuaded Jack to leave the farm and drove him in Nigel's car to the hospital.

Carys, having volunteered to be driver over the weekend, was now sadly returning the keys to the Manor. With a few words of thanks and politely refusing an offer of coffee, she too made her way out of the village. She hadn't met Nigel, but she could well understand the boys feeling bewildered. She felt it too and was struggling to keep her emotions in check and concentrate on her driving. She knew she had to try and stay strong to help Nick and his family through this very difficult time, but increasingly she was fearful about where it would all end.

She found Gina with the little girls in the waiting room, who told her the others were with Ruth. Not wanting to intrude, Carys joined in entertaining Sophie and Paige, glad of the distraction. Gina was quietly able to convey to her that Emma had been able to identify the cap as Nigel's and, exchanging knowing glances and fingers crossed, they both hoped this would lead to the final chapter of this dreadful ordeal.

Chapter 24

Nick and Jack sat on one side of the bed with Rob and Emma on the other; all of them patiently waiting for Ruth to wake up. They would have to gauge carefully whether she was able to cope with the latest news, as the nurses were still concerned about her fragility.

Eventually, she opened her eyes and smiled when she saw everyone.

Taking Emma's hand, she said, "I'm glad you're all here as I have something to tell you."

Everyone leaned forward as her voice was barely above a whisper.

"Your Dad came to visit me last night. He's so sorry he couldn't stay for the party, but sends you all his love."

Emma said, "Oh Mum," and squeezed Ruth's hand willing the others not to say anything. Clearly her mother was still very confused. "Can someone tell the nurse Mum's awake?"

Rob got up, but Jack beat him to the door saying, "I'll go," and disappeared.

"Go after him," Nick nodded to Rob.

"It's such a shame," they heard Ruth say, "particularly for Jack, having come all this way and not even seeing his dad."

"Mum - he's missing remember?" Nick said gently as Emma blinked back her tears.

"I know," Ruth replied, still with a tremor in her voice. "It's difficult to even think about living without him, but we have to stay strong and keep his memory alive."

A nurse came into the room then and smiling at Ruth said, "I'm sure you feel much better now after a good sleep. Can I get you anything? A cup of tea perhaps?"

"That would be lovely, thank you."

Nick and Emma were astonished. They could hardly believe what they were hearing. Maybe her restless night and strange comments were because of the medication. She must be on stronger painkillers and a more substantial sedative. Nick followed the nurse as she left the ward and asked her. He was really worried about how best to deal with his mother's state of mind.

"Your mother is on painkillers and she was given a mild sedative last night when she became so distressed, but I doubt they will have made her confused. She probably had a bad dream and is it any wonder with all that's gone on? I wouldn't pursue what's she's saying just now. Leave it until after her op tomorrow. Hopefully things will become clearer in a day or two. We'll be keeping a close eye on her, so please try not to worry."

She left Nick to get Ruth her cup of tea. He returned to the ward where he found Emma still holding her mother's hand and looking so sad.

"Em, can you come and see the girls a minute please? Won't be a sec Mum."

Outside the room Nick told Emma what the nurse had said and she was quite relieved there would be no follow-up on the subject of her missing father for now. She was still reeling from his cap being found and dreading what else would be discovered.

"It's been such an ordeal for poor Mum. It's really not surprising she's having nightmares. I'll stay with her for a bit longer, but will you get Rob to take the girls home please? They've been here long enough and I don't think she's up to seeing them today."

"Of course, and Carrie or I will give you a lift when you're ready to leave."

Emma went back to her mother and Nick went to find Rob. He wasn't in the waiting room and Carys told him he'd gone after Jack who'd run off down the corridor. Nick found the two men outside. Jack was leaning against the wall, looking up at the sky, and clearly very upset with Rob doing his best to console him.

Nick put his arm round his younger brother saying, "Come on buddy, let's find a quiet corner to sort this out."

As he led Jack back inside the hospital, he said to Rob, "Emma wants you to take the girls home please Rob. Carrie or I will give her a lift later."

"Thanks," Rob said and followed Jack and Nick to the waiting room. He got the girls into their coats and they said goodbye.

Gina and Carys could see Jack was distressed and tactfully left them to get coffees.

Quietly, Nick closed the door behind them and turning to Jack said, "Let it go Jack."

The flood gates opened then and they both sobbed. When they were able to regain their composure, Nick told Jack what the nurse had said.

"It's best just to forget what Mum was saying. She had a bad dream and it's left her a bit muddled. Hopefully, once she's had the operation and we can get her home, she'll be more lucid. Let's try and cheer up and see how she's doing."

Pulling themselves together, the two men returned to the ward to find Emma still looking very concerned, but their mother was much brighter, having had something to eat.

"You really don't need to stay. I'll be fine. Why don't you all go home? I'll see you tomorrow after my op."

"We'll stay a bit longer,' Nick said firmly. "Emma why don't you join Carrie and Gina for a coffee? Jack and I'll keep Mum company."

Emma shot him a look as though she was going to object, but then changed her mind, "I won't be long; I could do with a drink."

She left the room and Jack took her place by the bed. Ruth put out her hand and Jack held it, clearly struggling to hold back the tears and not daring to look his mother in the face.

"What time is the op tomorrow?" Nick asked trying to make conversation.

"First thing, I think. I'm top of the list apparently. I'll be glad to get it over and done with."

"How long afterwards will you have to stay in hospital?" Nick continued.

"Not long hopefully, if everything goes according to plan. I'll be glad to get home. Jack, will you be staying for a while longer?"

Jack looked up then and said croakily, "I've got nothing to rush back to Australia for - I can stay as long as you'll have me."

Ruth smiled at him and squeezed his hand. Nick realised he hadn't given Jack's return any thought at all and was relieved to know he would be staying, at least for a while.

Emma found Gina and Carys in the cafe sitting at a table by the window.

"May I join you?"

"Of course," Carys said, "how's your mum?"

Emma explained to them what her mother had said about their dad.

"We can't make it out. It's as if she knows what's happened to him, but the nurses think she's just had a vivid dream."

"Stress can play tricks," Carys said, "I was awake last night and looked out the window. There was a funny light, casting weird shadows over the woods and I saw, what I thought was a bat or an owl, but it looked so much bigger. Then it just disappeared; it must have been a figment of my imagination."

Gina immediately made the connection to what Kevin had told her about what the old man had said to Rob, but not wanting to raise any further alarm, she said hastily, "It's no wonder you're all upset. It's been a dreadful time."

"I think I'd better get back to Mum,' Emma said anxiously. "I left Jack and Nick with her, but I'm not sure they're coping very well."

"Do you think I should stay with them at the house tonight, Emma?" Carys asked. "I don't really want to drive home on my own this evening and I can leave first thing to get to work."

"That would be great Carrie, thank you."

"I can take over in the morning,' Gina said, "unless you want me to stay too?"

"That's kind of you Gina, but I think we'll manage. Can I call you if we need you?"

"Of course, anytime and I'll let you know if I hear anything from Kevin or Dan."

She had been expecting an update, but obviously there was nothing to report and the search would likely be called off again soon as it was getting dark. She would phone Kevin to see what was happening and report this latest revelation before heading home.

The women left the cafe together; Carys and Emma returning to Ruth and Gina going outside to make the call.

Chapter 25

The narrow path was very overgrown and clearing it was difficult. The farmers had taken in turns all day using a variety of tools from strimmers to hedge clippers, but with darkness falling, they would have to stop.

Kevin had been helping to shift the undergrowth as it was cut away, but was now making for the pub to report off duty. He would have a lager shandy and call Gina to see how the family were doing and tell her nothing more had been found. He had almost reached the Unit when his phone rang and he saw it was her.

"Hi Gina. I'm afraid there's nothing new to report here. How's everything your end?"

"Not great. Apparently, Mrs Harrison had a strange dream about her husband visiting her and understandably, everyone is very upset. Also, Carys mentioned, when she was awake last night, she looked out the window and saw something fly out of the wood on a beam of light! It vanished, so she put it down to stress and imagining it, but it sounds awfully similar to what the old chap said don't you think?"

"I do and I'm beginning to think there's a lot more to discover about Nigel Harrison's disappearance. I'll let Dan know what you've said, but he's a bit sceptical about there being anything creepy going on."

"I don't want to believe it either, but the mystery remains."

"Let's hope we find Nigel Harrison soon and get some answers. Are you going home?"

"Yes, but I've said they can call me at any time and I'll go to the house first thing in the morning."

"Thanks, I'll let Dan know and be in touch tomorrow."

They rang off, each relieved to get a little downtime, although still well aware of the gravity of the situation and the family's suffering.

Chapter 26

At the hospital, Nick, Emma and Jack were tearfully saying goodnight to their mother. Carys too, had a lump in her throat as she watched them and blew a kiss from the door. She wanted to give them time as a family and went to get her coat from the waiting room. She found Gina there, who told her there was nothing new from Kevin. Carys thanked her and they said goodbye.

Nick was to drive Emma home and Jack would go with Carys to show her the way to the Harrison's house. It would be another long night, but maybe easier to bear being in familiar surroundings.

Jack said very little on the journey and had to be prompted several times about which way to go. Carys understood his need for reflection. His homecoming had been anything but a joyous reunion. She had heard from Gina about his feelings of guilt and wondered whether returning to the family home would make things better or worse.

Jack told her to take the next on the right which turned out to be a narrow lane winding its way up a steep hill.

"Just round the next bend, you'll see a driveway on your left - that's it."

Carys turned into the drive and immediately security lights came on over the double garage and porch, shining over a neat front garden. Carys' first impression was that it wasn't a particularly big house, but still very impressive. As she swung the car round to park, Jack spotted something.

"What the..?" he began and opened the car door before Carys could stop. Sprinting across the drive to the porch, he went down on his knees, "Brodie?" he said looking at the almost lifeless body.

Carys dug in her pocket to retrieve the key Nick had given her and opened the front door. She was fumbling to find a light switch, but Jack had already picked the dog up and was charging down the hall to the rear of the house. He knew his way, even in the dark, and took the stricken animal through the kitchen to a utility room where there was a shower. Carefully, he laid Brodie on the floor and taking his clothes off down to his underpants, put on the light and ran the water.

"Come on Brodie, you need to get cleaned up," he said, trying to sound positive.

He didn't think the dog was seriously hurt, but he was filthy, wet, and shivering. If he got him in the shower, it would warm him up and he would be able to see if there were any injuries. Brodie remained lying down, not even able to lift his head, but there was a slight quiver of his tail.

This gave Jack hope and he tried again, "Come on Brodie, good boy. Let's get you sorted."

Still the dog didn't move.

Jack got his arms under the still shivering dog and gently took him into the shower where the water washed over them both splashing mud everywhere. Jack knelt down and carefully lowered the dog, before feeling all over his body and down his legs to see if he was wounded. Brodie offered no resistance to this and Jack could not find anything obvious. There was no sign of blood as the water continued to run over them and with Jack making reassuring noises, the dog seemed to relax a little.

"Come on Brodie, up you get."

The dog still lay there, although he did raise his head briefly and thump his tail.

"That's it - you can do it. Come on Brodie."

Carys found towels and spread them on the floor just outside the shower. She knew very little about dogs, having not been brought up with them, but she loved animals and could see the very special bond Jack still had with Brodie.

Once again, Jack carefully put his arms under the dog's body and lifted him out of the shower and onto the towels. Gently he rubbed the sodden fur whilst talking quietly to the animal.

"I don't think he can be really hurt or he'd be yelping and complaining about being moved. Maybe he was hit by a car and it's left him paralysed, but then how did he get here? Maybe he's just exhausted and hungry. Are you starving boy – is that it?"

Brodie managed a couple of thumps from his tail as an answer.

"I'll get him something," Carys offered, "what will he eat?"

Jack looked at her with a wry smile and said, "He's a Labrador - he'll eat anything! But perhaps scrambled egg or porridge?"

"I'll get the bags from the car and see what we've got."

Jack continued talking soothingly, whilst gently rubbing Brodie's limp body. Carys returned with food bags and Jack's backpack which she took through to him.

"You'll likely want to change out of those wet pants," she said and went to look through the food they had brought back with them.

She found eggs, milk and half a loaf of bread as well as bacon, butter, and cereal. There would be plenty for them all to have supper and breakfast she thought, as she whisked the eggs.

On her way down the hall with Brodie's bowl, Carys heard a knocking on the front door and saw Nick peering through the porch window. Being very relieved to see him, she quickly let him in and explained what had happened. A look of disbelief came over Nick's face as he strode down the hall to the utility room where Jack was tucking his shirt into his trousers, still looking at Brodie, full of concern.

"How is he?"

At the sound of Nick's voice, the dog looked up and weakly wagged his tail.

"I don't really know. He doesn't appear to be really injured, but I'm worried he's got something going on internally and wonder if we should try and get him to a vet tonight."

"I think we should. I'll see if I can find a number for one locally."

Nick punched the information required into his mobile and pressed the number listed. Inevitably, there was another number to call in an emergency, and he had to go through the procedure again after he had found a pen and paper.

Meanwhile, the scrambled eggs had cooled sufficiently and Jack was trying to tempt Brodie to eat. The dog made a half-hearted attempt to lick the food from Jack's hand, but even that was too much effort and with a resigned grunt, he lay his head down again.

Nick was giving their address, having explained the circumstances for Brodie's condition and when he rang off, he said, "The vet's coming here. He shouldn't be long."

Jack sat on the floor beside Brodie stroking his head. Nick went to join him. Neither of them had grown up with the dog, but he was very much a part of their family. They knew Ruth and Nigel, as well as Emma, Rob and the little girls would be absolutely devastated if Brodie didn't recover. To lose the dog now did not bear thinking about.

Carys was making mugs of tea when the doorbell rang and she went to answer it. The vet was a very young man and completely different to the image she had of a Vet, but he had an air of confidence about him as she led him down the hallway heading for his patient.

"Hi," he said to Jack and Nick, who stood up to give him room to take a look at Brodie. "What's happened to you old chap?"

"We don't really know. He went missing with my father last Friday in Bentley Wood," Nick explained. "My father still hasn't been found, but somehow Brodie has made his way here. Goodness knows how because he doesn't seem able to move."

The vet examined Brodie as best he could with him lying down, and confirmed he didn't think he had any broken bones, but noticed his pads looked sore and some front claws looked jagged.

"It looks as though he's been digging or walked a long way. He's probably exhausted or worst-case scenario, hurt his back and it's gone into spasm. I'll give him an injection and if he's no better in the morning, you'll need to take him to the surgery so they can do an x-ray and see what's going on."

Brodie lay still whilst the treatment was administered and raised his head to lick the hand that was making a fuss of him.

"If only you could tell your story," the vet said quietly, "then we might be able to find your master."

Brodie responded lethargically and, with a final rub behind his ears, the vet got up to leave.

"Will you phone the surgery in the morning, even if he's recovered. I'd like to know how he is."

"Of course," Nick said, "and thank you for coming out - it's much appreciated."

They all said good night and continued their vigil.

Eventually, Nick murmured to Carys, "You should really get some rest. You've got to drive into town first thing for work."

"I'm OK, but I wish you'd eat something. What about cheese on toast?"

"That'd be good," Nick replied, but without even looking at Jack, knew he would need to be persuaded.

Carys made supper, which they ate, almost in silence, whilst still keeping a watchful eye on Brodie, who seemed to be sleeping peacefully.

Nick showed Carys to their room for the night before going back downstairs with a duvet and pillow, which he put on the settee in the living room, suggesting to Jack that they carry Brodie through on his bed; then one of them could stay up with him, but at least be comfortable. Jack agreed and between them they managed to carefully lift the still sleeping dog. The wood burner was laid and Nick put a match to it, not that the house was cold, but it made a warm glow in the big room.

Jack insisted he stay with Brodie and Nick did not argue. He felt exhausted, but knew he probably wouldn't sleep. Carys was already in bed and he was grateful for her presence.

Downstairs Jack got under the duvet and for the first time since his return, he felt at home.

Chapter 27

Jack was woken by a soft touch on his hand and a cold wet nose on his. He blinked and took a minute to remember where he was and all that had happened. Again, a nudge and he realised it was Brodie, on his feet, tail wagging and clearly needing to be let outside.

"Oh Brodie - thank goodness you're OK."

Jack ruffled the dog's ears and got up. The pair padded through the kitchen to the back door. It was barely light and Jack could not believe he'd been so sound asleep. He put the kettle on to boil and looked in the fridge and cupboards to see what he could give Brodie, knowing he must be hungry. He found the dried food he usually had, but thought he should probably have something lighter and set about making scrambled eggs.

As Jack let Brodie in from his patrol around the garden, Nick appeared looking bleary-eyed and having obviously slept in his clothes. He couldn't keep the smile from his face when Brodie greeted him and he got down on the floor to give him a proper fuss.

"Oh, look at you Brodie boy - it's so good to see you're alright. He looks great, doesn't he? I just wish he could tell us what's happened to Dad."

Jack gave Brodie the bowl of scrambled eggs and they both watched the dog in silence. It took only seconds for it to be demolished and Brodie showed his appreciation by wagging his tail and wrapping himself around the two men wanting to be petted. They heard Carys coming downstairs and before they could say anything, Brodie was trotting into the hall to make her acquaintance.

"Well, hello, looks like you've made a good recovery."

She too stroked and patted him, relieved this was one concern that seemed to have come to a happy conclusion.

"I must get on the road, but I'll try and get back tonight."

She kissed them both goodbye and all three went to see her off.

Back in the house, Nick went to have a shower and change his clothes, whilst Jack prepared to cook bacon and eggs for their breakfast. Brodie's recovery, and a surprisingly good night's sleep, had given him clarity. He realised he would have to be more optimistic if he was going to ably support the rest of the family.

Emma arrived to an elated welcome from Brodie. In disbelief, she made a big fuss of him as she listened to Jack and Nick telling her what they could and she scolded them for not phoning to let her know.

"We didn't want to worry you Em," Nick told her, "and it was pretty late by the time the vet had been."

"I wonder what Mum will say? Finding Brodie on the doorstep is amazing, but we still have to find Dad. I rang the hospital first thing and they said she had a reasonably good night. No more nightmares anyway. She'd had her pre-med and was about to go to theatre. I said I'd phone again later to see how she's doing."

There was a knock at the front door and Brodie, tail wagging, trotted down the hallway as eager as ever to see who was there. It was Gina who was clearly astounded to be greeted by a big black dog she thought was missing. She looked at Jack, clearly puzzled by this latest development and he explained to her what had happened.

She immediately relayed the information to Kevin who was once again on duty at the Unit.

"I guess it's good news the dog's found his way home, but we're still no nearer to finding Mr Harrison. If only the dog could speak, we might make some real progress."

They ended their call and Gina joined the siblings, gratefully accepting a cup of coffee. She certainly thought Jack had a more positive attitude and looked a little less troubled than he had the day before. Brodie turning up would be giving them all hope that Nigel would be found too, but as the dog's whereabouts had not been reported during his journey home, no one had any idea which route he had taken.

The search had been widened each day with larger areas of farmland being covered on the ground, as well as by a helicopter in the air. In less rural places, house to house enquiries had been made and appeals put out over the radio and on television. Still no sightings had been reported. Nigel Harrison's disappearance remained a mystery.

Chapter 28

They were leaving the house for the hospital, when Gina received a call from Kevin. The cadaver dog had alerted her handler to a rectangular patch of peaty earth that could so easily have been overlooked. It was now being investigated.

Gina really wasn't sure whether or not to impart this latest bit of information. There was absolutely nothing conclusive and she didn't want to alarm anyone unnecessarily or raise their hopes, only to have them dashed if the discovery proved to be unconnected. The family had already left, so she decided to keep it to herself for now and wait to see what Kevin's next call would reveal.

She didn't have long to wait and was able to pull over to answer her phone.

"What's happening Kevin?"

"I think Mr Harrison has been found. A body has been recovered matching his description. Obviously, we'll need someone to formally identify him and I hate to put the family through that, but it's the only way to know for certain."

Even though the outcome had been looking less and less likely to be favourable as time went on, it was nevertheless a very sad ending. Gina confessed to Kevin that she hadn't told the family about the possible finding and was still somewhat reluctant to burden them with another pressure when their mother was going through an operation. Kevin offered to drive over to the hospital and share the responsibility.

Nick, Emma and Jack were all sat in the tiny waiting room, saying very little. They had been told Ruth's operation had gone well and she was now in the recovery room. They would be called in as soon as she was compos mentis.

They were immediately wary when they saw Kevin and Gina together, and correctly assumed they had bad news.

"We think we've found your father," Kevin told them gently, "but I'm afraid not alive."

Even though they had almost been expecting this outcome, the grim reality was hard to take in and their despair was obvious as they clung to each other for support.

"A body has been found in Bentley Woods and matches his description," Kevin said sadly, "I'm so very sorry."

Considerately, he gave them a few minutes to try and come to terms with this tragic turn of events before saying, "We'll need someone to formally identify him."

"I'll do it," Nick volunteered without hesitation and Jack readily agreed to go with him.

Emma said nothing, but faced her brothers and shook her head, "I can't do it, I'm sorry. I want to remember Dad as I last saw him, not having been dug up out of the ground!" She sobbed, visibly shaking with emotion.

Kevin thanked them and said he would let them know once arrangements were made at the morgue. He left them then, to let Dan know the family had been notified, and that Nick and Jack were prepared to attend the identification.

Gina was impressed by their strength and courage, but knew behind their brave faces, their hearts were broken.

"Do you think we should tell Mum?" Jack asked.

"I think we should leave it until we know for sure, and when she's recovered from surgery," Emma answered quickly and Nick agreed.

The nurse came in to say Ruth was ready for visitors, but asked them not to stay too long. Ruth was propped up on pillows, her leg in a cast and slightly elevated. She looked remarkably well, considering she had just had an operation, and smiled when she saw them all.

"It's over, thank goodness and now I just want to get home. How are you all doing?"

"We're OK Mum," Emma said, "and we have some news."

The boys looked startled, but then she said, "Brodie has managed to find his way back home - isn't that incredible?"

"Oh, my goodness, that's amazing - is he alright?"

"He's fine," Jack told her. "We had the vet out last night because we weren't sure, but he seems fully recovered now."

"Your Dad never went anywhere without Brodie and he'll miss him."

Again, her children were alarmed by what she was saying, but no one commented or encouraged her to explain further. There would be a more appropriate time to unravel her meanderings. Meanwhile, it was imperative to keep her calm, despite their inner turmoil.

When they returned to Gina in the waiting room, she had heard from Dan that the body was at the morgue. She was to let him know when the boys were going to be there, so he or Kevin could meet them. Gina offered to drive them, knowing full well that identifying a dead body was an ordeal and would be a traumatising experience. However, in the event, Dan sent a patrol car to take them, enabling Gina to remain at the hospital with Emma and Ruth.

Chapter 29

The brothers spoke very little during their journey to the mortuary. There, they were met by Dan and Kevin who shook their hands warmly, trying to reassure them about the unpleasant task ahead. They were introduced to the mortuary assistant, a kindly middle-aged lady, who tried to prepare them for what they were about to face, before showing them through to the viewing room.

Both men knew this was going to be the most difficult thing either of them had ever done. Nick felt he had absolutely no choice and must do it as the eldest. Jack having said he would do it to support Nick, was inwardly panicking that he might not even recognise his father, having really not seen him for quite a few years.

"Ready?" the assistant asked.

They both nodded and the curtains were drawn back. Their dismay was palpable. Apart from an obvious contusion on his forehead, his skin was like porcelain, an empty shell. The life, the spirit, the soul had left him - Nigel Harrison was no more.

In unison, they turned away. Any hopes they may have had, that perhaps it would not turn out to be their father after all, completely shattered. Undeniably that body, lying totally lifeless on a slab in the morgue was their dad, Nigel Harrison.

Returning to the waiting room, they were both struggling with their emotions. Indeed, Jack thought he was going to be sick. Nick grabbed him in an effort to control his own feelings and Jack returned the powerful embrace. They were respectfully left to overcome their grief.

Without asking, cups of tea were provided, laced with sugar, giving everyone time to regain their composure.

Eventually, Kevin said, "A post mortem will have to be carried out to establish the cause of death and until then, your father's body will have to remain at the morgue."

Nick and Jack dumbly nodded, as if understanding, but Kevin recognised their fear and bewilderment. How would they or the rest of the family, ever come to terms with such a tragedy?

The two men were driven back to the hospital and shakily told Emma and Gina that it was indeed, Nigel who had been found. The brothers and sister clung together, desperately trying to summon up the courage to tell their mother.

Gina quietly asked them if they would like her to impart the devastating news, but they all agreed to do it together. If Nick and Jack thought identifying their father's body was difficult, then telling Ruth he was dead, was going to be incredibly tough.

Nick told the nurse on duty to make sure she was aware, and get her opinion on whether Ruth, so soon after surgery, would be strong enough to take it. The nurse

116

reassured him that it was better for her to know sooner rather than later, and not run the risk of her hearing about it from someone else.

The three of them filed in very solemnly to see Ruth. She looked much better. Her face had lost its pallor and her eyes were brighter as she smiled at them all.

Emma was the first to speak, "We have some very sad news, Mum. Dad has been found, but he's dead!" Her voice, caught in a sob, as she went to embrace her mother.

Ruth looked at the boys and held out her free hand to them. They went to her and all four gripped each other.

"Do we know what happened to him?" Ruth said eventually through her tears.

Nick shook his head, "Not yet - there has to be a post mortem."

"Where was he found?"

Jack this time responded quickly by saying, "In the wood; somehow he must've strayed from the main footpath and fell, hitting his head."

His tone relayed to the others not to enlighten their mother with any further details, which they understood.

Because of the extraordinarily tragic circumstances, the family were allowed to come and go as they pleased. Emma was offered a bed, so she could stay with her mother until she could be discharged from hospital.

Chapter 30

Kevin appeared at the house a few days later with the Coroner's Officer to give them the result of the post mortem. Nigel Harrison had suffered a severe blow to his head and a fatal heart attack. It was difficult to establish if the one caused the other or in what order.

"It's unlikely he knew anything about it," the Coroner's Officer told them kindly, "but how he came to be so neatly buried in the wood remains a mystery. Forensics are still looking for clues, but the surrounding area is still very wet, making the recovery of anything substantial nigh on impossible. A Coroner's enquiry will take place once we've received the forensics report, but it looks very much as though the verdict will be accidental death or natural causes."

The family thanked Kevin sincerely for all his efforts. They had come to rely on his quiet determination and calm presence. Their lives would never be the same again, but he too had clearly been deeply affected by the extraordinary events surrounding Nigel Harrison's disappearance and subsequent death.

Ruth had received an ecstatic welcome from Brodie when she had been discharged home and, although she was incredibly sad to have lost her beloved husband in such tragic circumstances, she realised life had to go on, somehow, without him. She was thankful that, at least for the time being, Jack would be staying at the house. He'd nowhere else to go and Ruth could see a developing friendship between him and Gina, who was still a regular visitor.

Nick and Carys were very obviously committed to one another and their long-term future.

Emma, Rob, and their little girls would miss Nigel dreadfully, but everyone talked about him with fondness and remembered him with pride.

This was a family in mourning, but they would cling together and stay strong. They would never know exactly what happened to Nigel, and maybe that was just as well.

The Listeners

By Walter De La Mare

'Is there anybody there?' said the Traveller,

Knocking on the moonlit door;

And his horse in the silence champed the grasses

Of the forest's ferny floor;

And a bird flew up out of the turret,

Above the Traveller's head;

And he smote upon the door a second time;

'Is there anybody there?' he said.

But no one descended to the Traveller;

No head from the leaf-fringed sill

Leaned over and looked into his grey eyes,

Where he stood perplexed and still.

But only a host of phantom listeners

That dwelt in the lone house then

Stood listening in the quiet of the moonlight

To that voice from the world of men:

Stood thronging the faint moonbeams on the dark stair,

That goes down to the empty hall,

Hearkening in an air stirred and shaken

By the lonely Traveller's call.

And he felt in his heart their strangeness,

Their stillness answering his cry,

While his horse moved, cropping the dark turf,

'Neath the starred and leafy sky;

For he suddenly smote on the door, even

Louder, and lifted his head -

'Tell them I came, and no one answered,

That I kept my word' he said.

Never the least stir made the listeners,

Though every word he spake

Fell echoing through the shadowiness of the still house

From the one man left awake:

Ay, they heard his foot upon the stirrup,

And the sound of iron on stone,

And how the silence surged softly backwards,

When the plunging hoofs were gone.

Printed in Great Britain
by Amazon

29069526R00076